# Sammy Carducci's
# GUIDE TO **W**OMEN

# ALSO BY RONALD KIDD

That's What Friends Are For
Dunker
Who Is Felix the Great?
Sizzle and Splat
The Glitch
Second Fiddle: A Sizzle and Splat Mystery

# Sammy Carducci's
## GUIDE TO WOMEN

## RONALD KIDD

LODESTAR BOOKS
Dutton                    New York

Copyright © 1991 by Ronald Kidd

*Library of Congress Cataloging-in-Publication Data*
Kidd, Ronald.
Sammy Carducci's Guide to women / Ronald Kidd.
   p.   cm.
Summary: A four-foot-two sixth grader gets pointers from his handsome older brother on handling women, and tries them out on a classmate.
ISBN 0-525-67363-6
[1. Dating (Social customs)—Fiction. 2. Humorous stories.]
I. Title. II. Title: Guide to women.
PZ7.K5315Sam   1991
[Fic]—dc20                                                    91-26588
                                                                  CIP
                                                                   AC

Published in the United States by Lodestar Books,
an affiliate of Dutton Children's Books,
a division of Penguin Books USA Inc.,
375 Hudson Street, New York, New York 10014

Published simultaneously in Canada
by McClelland & Stewart, Toronto

Editor: Rosemary Brosnan
Designer: Richard Granald, LMD

Printed in the U.S.A.
First Edition
10  9  8  7  6  5  4  3  2  1

To Greg Martin, Stephanie Bonello Martin,
and my Italian in-laws,
with gratitude
for creating the greatest Italian dish of all—
Yvonne

# CONTENTS

# Sammy Carducci's
# GUIDE TO WOMEN

# 1

# THE MAN

🖊 Sammy

First off, there's my name. It's Samuele Lorenzo Carducci. A real mouthful, right? Sounds like something you'd order with clam sauce, if you could just figure out how to say it. So I'll give you a break. You can call me Sammy.

Then there's my size—a towering four feet two. A lot of people would call that short. But hey, I don't look at it that way. I say it's all a state of mind. Me, I feel tall.

Every once in a while, somebody comes along who disagrees. "Hey, shrimp," they might say.

"That's Mr. Shrimp to you," I tell them. Then I unwrap a stick of gum and calmly slide it in my mouth. I might even offer them one, so they know they're dealing with a class act.

Of course, that should already be obvious because of how I dress. I'm the only kid in my sixth-grade class who wears a suit. I also wear a tie, and on test days I'll slip a red handkerchief in my pocket. I usually finish off the outfit with a pair of black high-top sneakers, just to show I haven't lost touch with the people. Unusual? Sure it is. That's why

I dress that way. Like my brother, Nick, says, it makes a statement.

I'm Italian, in case the name didn't tip you off. Or at least half Italian. My grandma and grandpa came over from Italy, only they called it the old country. Funny thing is, when I was younger, I didn't understand what they meant. I thought the old country was a place where everybody was old, just like my grandparents.

My grandma has lived with us ever since my grandpa died. She may be old, but she's not one of those shriveled-up grandmothers you sometimes see. Her nose is big and her chin's strong, and she's even got a pretty good pair of shoulders on her. These days she mostly watches the soaps and makes spaghetti. I like to help her in the kitchen because first of all, I'm a spaghetti freak, and second of all, she's great to talk to.

"You nice boy, Sammy," she says, watching me cut up green peppers. Her accent is thick, like the tomato sauce we're making. "Just one thing I don't understand. Why you wearing that suit?"

"I gotta look good, Grandma," I tell her.

"You look crazy."

"You think Nick looks crazy?"

Nick graduated from high school last year. He works in an insurance office and dresses sharp.

"Nickie got to have suits," she says. "He works at a desk."

"So do I," I shoot back, grinning.

She shakes her head. "What am I gonna do with you, Sammy?"

"Make spaghetti, just like always."

2

My dad is Italian, but my mom isn't. I think her people are from England or Sweden. Anyway, it's a place where they don't talk very loud. Her family is amazing to watch. When they get together in a room, they just sit there. Somebody might cough and then say something in a voice you can barely hear. Everybody nods; then it gets quiet again.

Once we made the mistake of inviting them to Thanksgiving dinner with my dad's family. To start with, they were outnumbered because there are lots of Carduccis. There was a size difference, too. It got so bad that some of my mom's smaller relatives were almost trampled. Even the ones who stayed out of the way were scared because people kept coming up and talking loud and waving their hands in the air.

Somehow that stuff has never bothered my mom. In fact, I think she likes it. After all, she married my dad, and he's about as Carducci as they come. Which means he talks in a booming voice and has an opinion on everything.

My mom, on the other hand, is short, with curly brown hair and a smile that sneaks up on you. She's quiet most of the time, but when you get to know her, you find out there's plenty going on inside. Besides, she's learned to speak up when she has something to say. Like the time she decided to get a job, for instance.

"You what?" says my dad when she tells him. He's used to making most of the decisions, whether he's home or at his construction company.

"You heard me, Joe," says my mom, knitting in front of the TV. "I'll be doing books part-time up at Green's Laundry."

"What about the family?"

"Sammy's at school. Nick's got a job. Grandma's got her TV set. They don't need me at home all day."

He starts to argue with her, but something in her eyes stops him.

"Joe, I'm going to do this," she says. And sure enough, she does.

My dad doesn't lose too many arguments. The only other big one I remember was with Nick. Come to think of it, that was about a job, too. On high school graduation day, Nick told my dad he'd been hired by an insurance company.

"You what?" my dad demands. It's one of his favorite sayings.

"I'm going to be a sales trainee," answers Nick, brushing his hair in front of the mirror. "In a few months I'll be doing commission sales. That's where the really big money is."

My dad puts his hands on his hips and looks away. When he looks back, he says, "And what about college?"

"Come on, Pop, that's the slow track. Four years of no salary. Besides, it's not like we're talking Harvard. The only school that would take me was the community college, and their degree's barely worth the paper it's printed on."

"You're wrong, Nickie. You're wrong about a lot of things."

Nick puts down the brush. "I'm sorry, Pop, but it's my life. I withdrew my application to school and took the job. I start in two weeks."

There's a lot of discussion after that, but when the dust settles, Nick goes to work, not to college. They agree he'll live at home as long as he pays rent.

That was almost a year ago. A few months later, when

4

Nick pulls up to the house in a brand-new Grand Am, I figure he made the right decision. As usual.

He's a pretty smooth customer, my brother. I guess part of it is that he looks good and knows it. He's got wavy black hair and olive-colored skin, with dark eyes that look sad the first time you see them. Women love staring into those eyes. I know because I've seen them do it.

It's not just his looks, though. He's got a way of talking that makes you think you're the most important person in the world. It even comes across on the telephone. Last week, for instance, Nick is on the phone in his room, and my best friend, Gus Gaffney, and I just happen to be in my room, right next door. It's not like we're listening in, but the walls are sort of thin, especially around the electrical outlets.

"Hey, come on, it's my turn," Gus whines.

I'm crouched down on the floor with my ear next to the outlet. "Ssh. I'm trying to concentrate."

Gus points to his clunky black plastic watch. "You've been concentrating for three minutes and fifty-five seconds. We were going to change every two minutes."

Gus has the honor of being the only kid in Mrs. McNulty's sixth-grade class with a smaller chest than mine. Not that he's that short. He's just unbelievably skinny. His arms and legs look like sticks, and when he pulls his belt tight, his jeans stick out in big loops around his waist. Some of the wise guys at school like to sneak up behind him and drop pennies down his pants. Gus doesn't mind, though. He says he can use the money.

"You know, Cindy," says Nick in the next room, "did I ever tell you how terrific you are?" I can just about feel this Cindy melting on the other end of the line. "No, I'm serious," he goes on. "The first time I saw you I felt, like, this incredible rush. It wasn't just the way you look, which by the way is sensational. It was more of, I don't know, a vibe, like this is a person I could really get close to."

I turn to Gus. "Is that great, or what?"

"What did he say?" asks Gus, frantically trying to push me away from the outlet.

"Hey, relax," I say. I move aside, adjusting the cuffs on my shirt.

Gus scrambles down on his knees and plasters his ear to the wall. He listens for a few seconds, then sits back and sighs. "He hung up. Just my luck."

"The man is poetry in motion," I say.

"I wouldn't know," says Gus, getting to his feet.

Just then Nick comes out of his room and walks past my door.

"Hey, Nick," I say, "how's it going?"

"Great. What are you two pipsqueaks up to?"

"Nothing much. Hey, what's the latest with that girl you've been going out with? Cindy, I think it is."

He looks at me kind of sideways. "I never told you her name."

"Nick, I'm your brother. Of course you told me her name. We got no secrets, you and me."

He laughs, then bends down and ruffles my hair. "You are one strange little kid." He looks over at Gus. "Make that two strange little kids." Gus raises his head into ruffling position, but Nick doesn't notice.

"Just for your information," Nick tells me, "Cindy and I are tight. Like this." He crosses one finger over the other

6

and squeezes them together. Then he grins and moves off down the hall.

"Wow, he really is poetry in motion," says Gus.

"Hey," I say, "he's my brother."

We wander into the kitchen, where I open a tin of Italian cookies my grandma made. I grab a couple of handfuls and set up Gus and me at the kitchen table with two glasses of milk. I'm into my third cookie when I notice Gus hasn't even taken a bite of his first. He's picking off the sesame seeds, one by one, and stacking them into a neat pile in the middle of his napkin.

"What is this?" I say.

"I don't like sesame seeds. They taste funny."

"They're too little to taste funny."

"I have a sensitive stomach," he tells me.

Finally he bites into the cookie, then sets it off to one side and starts moving the seeds around on his napkin. He pushes them into a lopsided square, with a pile of extra seeds at each corner. I just stare at him.

"You gonna tell me what that is," I ask, "or do we have to play Twenty Questions?"

"It's a fort," he tells me without looking up. He takes another cookie, picks off a few more sesame seeds, and sets them inside the so-called fort. "These are U.S. Cavalry officers." He puts some other seeds over by the edge of the napkin. "These are Apache Indians."

I sigh and shake my head. "How long we been friends now, Gus?"

"A year or so."

"And you're still playing cowboys and Indians?"

He sits up straight. There's a worried look on his face,

like he gets when Mrs. McNulty calls on him in class. "Is something wrong with that?"

"Nothing, if you're satisfied with just being a kid."

"What are my other choices?"

"Well, there's manhood," I say.

Gus thinks about it for a minute. "What do I have to do?"

"For one thing, stop building forts out of sesame seeds."

He looks down at the napkin with a sad expression on his face. "Yeah? What else?"

"You might start thinking about women."

"You mean like Mrs. McNulty?"

"She's a teacher, not a woman. I'm talking Annie Bowers, Lisa Phipps, Janie Hodges."

"Janie Hodges?" says Gus. "The girl who sits next to me in class?"

"That's the one."

"She gives me the creeps. She's always drawing hearts on her notebook."

"Gus," I explain patiently, "that's the way women are. Hearts, flowers, mushy songs—they love that stuff."

"They do?"

"Have you ever noticed the way they act around that new teacher, Mr. Lawrence?"

"They giggle a lot," says Gus.

"They're in love. Giggling is one of the ten early warning signs."

I down another cookie, then pick up the phone directory and start thumbing through it. I find what I'm looking for in a few seconds.

"What are you doing?" asks Gus, reaching for his glass of milk.

I drag the phone over to the table and tap out a number. "You'll see."

There's a ringing on the other end of the line. "Hello," says a girl's voice.

"Is this Janie Hodges?" I ask.

Gus just about chokes on his milk. He starts coughing like a maniac.

"Yes, it is," she says. "Are you all right? Who is this?"

I cough a few times and clear my throat, waving for Gus to move away from the table. He scoots his chair back and hurries across the room, where he grabs a couple of paper towels and claps them over his mouth.

"This is Sammy Carducci," I tell her. "I just got something stuck in my throat. I think it might have been a piece of broccoli."

"If you want to copy my homework again, you can just forget it."

"Hey, did I say anything about homework? Matter of fact, I was calling about something of a more, shall we say, personal nature."

"I don't want to talk about anything personal with you."

"Janie," I say, throwing Gus a wink, "did I ever tell you how terrific you are?" Gus's eyes get big, and he starts coughing again.

"There's somebody in the room with you, isn't there?" says Janie. "This is getting weird, Sammy. I'm going to hang up."

"No, wait!" I say.

9

"I'll give you five seconds."

"The first time I saw you, I felt this incredible rush," I tell her. I try to act cool, but it's hard when you're talking as fast as you can. "I guess it might have been what you might call a vibe."

She starts giggling. I figure that's good, since giggling is one of the ten early warning signs of love. Then she bursts out laughing. That's not good. In fact, sometimes it's a warning sign of hate. Sure enough, there's a click, and the line goes dead.

When I set down the phone, Gus sprints back across the room, wiping his mouth on a paper towel. There's still some milk on one cheek, and a couple of sesame seeds are plastered on the side of his nose.

"Well?" he says.

"Not my type. She wanted to keep talking, but I figured it wouldn't be fair to her."

"So you just hung up?"

I shrug. "She'll thank me for it someday."

He looks at me like I'm some kind of movie star. "How did you think of all those things to tell her?"

"Instinct. You get a feeling for it."

"What if she had been your type, Sammy?"

"I was thinking of asking her to the dance," I say, calmly studying my nails.

He gets an expression like he just bit into a pickle. "You mean the one they're having for the sixth grade?"

"Oh, that's right, you wouldn't be interested," I say. "They aren't playing cowboys and Indians."

He straightens his shoulders. "I might be interested. I just don't know if I want to go with anybody."

10

"So go by yourself. That's what most people are doing."

"Are you planning to ask anybody else?" says Gus.

"I'll know in a few days. I'm doing a little survey to check out my other prospects."

Actually, there is no survey. The idea has just popped into my head. The more I think about it, though, the more it seems like a stroke of genius.

The problem with the call to Janie Hodges was lack of organization. Obviously, if I'd planned my moves better, she would have been thrilled to talk to me. What I need is a new approach based on scientific principles. A survey seems like the perfect way to start.

"Wow," says Gus, "do you think I could come along and help?"

"Sure," I tell him. "If you keep your nose clean, I might even give you a few pointers."

"I'll be good, Sammy, I promise."

"No, I mean wipe off your nose. Those sesame seeds are disgusting."

11

# THE WOMAN

✎ Becky

I<small>T WAS</small> a perfect fall afternoon. The sun was shining, the cool wind had turned warm, and kids were out playing all around the neighborhood. There was only one place for a healthy eleven-year-old girl to be on a day like this, and that's exactly where Alice and I were headed.

"I love the mall," she said as we pushed open the doors and walked inside. "It's got everything you'd ever want under one roof—clothes, makeup, VCRs, and boys."

Her name was Alice Biddle. Mine was Becky Davidson. And we were best friends, even though we weren't very much alike. I came from a happy, middle-class home in suburbia, where I lived with two loving parents, a parakeet, and a cocker spaniel. My family went to church on Sundays and really did eat white bread. Alice's home was the two-bedroom apartment her mother had rented after getting divorced, and the place was strewn with clothing and diet drink cans. Mrs. Biddle worked as a secretary during the week and a caterer's assistant on weekends. It was a very different world from mine, which was part of what attracted me to Alice.

"You talk about boys like they're something you can put in a bag and take home," I told her.

"I wish I could."

"That's what I like about you, Alice. The last of the great romantics."

"What does romance have to do with it?" she said. "I want a guy who's rich and good looking. The rest can be taught."

She stopped at the window of a lingerie store and, sighing, gazed wistfully at a mannequin. It was wearing a bra, something Alice had no need of.

"Don't worry," I said, "there are more important things in life."

"Yeah? Name two. Besides, Becky Davidson, you're not allowed to talk about it. Your chest is almost as big as my mother's."

"I just got an early start, that's all."

She laughed. "An early start? You've passed every other girl in the sixth grade and most of the ones in junior high, too."

Alice pulled me back a step from the window so she could study our reflections. "Look at us—Becky and the beast. You're five feet six, with blonde hair, blue eyes, and a figure that would make grown men cry."

"Alice—"

"I, on the other hand, have freckles and a mouthful of metal. I'm four feet eight and disappear when I turn sideways."

"You're very pretty," I said.

"Warped taste. It's your only shortcoming."

I had to laugh. I did a lot of that when I was around

Alice. We'd met on the first day of sixth grade, when we sat next to each other and discovered we were both new to the school. Alice told a joke to help me over my nervousness, and we'd been laughing together ever since.

"Admit it, Becky," said Alice as we made our way down the mall. "You're as interested in boys as I am."

"Maybe so. But not because of money and good looks."

"Come on, I've seen you making cow eyes at Mr. Lawrence, just like every other girl in class."

"Okay, he is good looking," I said. "But he has lots of other wonderful qualities."

"Such as?"

"He's kind and gentle. And he's a good listener. When you're talking to him, you know he really cares."

"I can go to my priest for that," she said.

"You talk tough, Alice, but you can't fool me. Deep down you're looking for love, just like everybody else."

She froze in her tracks, her eyes as big as saucers. It reminded me of the way our dog Beulah acts when she's spotted a bird.

"There he is," said Alice in hushed tones.

I followed her gaze to the part of the mall known as the food park, where you can buy everything from cookies to hot dogs on a stick. Sitting around one of the tables was a group of boys.

"There who is?" I asked.

"Don't stare!"

"Alice, you're the one who's staring!"

"I am?" She tore her gaze away and turned so her back was to the boys. "The one in the letterman's jacket with

14

the incredibly sexy blond hair. I know his name—It's Kevin Reynolds.''

"In the black jeans and loafers?"

"That's him. He goes to Brentwood Prep. My mom helped cater a party at his house last week."

He was about five feet eight, with a relaxed, easy manner. He had a great smile, which he used a lot, and Alice had been right about the hair.

"He is handsome," I said. "Isn't he a little old, though?"

"Fourteen. That's perfect. In ten years he'll be twenty-four and you'll be twenty-one."

"*I'll* be twenty-one? What's that supposed to mean?"

"Look, Becky, it's obvious I don't have a chance with Kevin. But you're perfect for him."

"Can we just leave?" I said.

"No, we need to get closer. Let's go buy a Coke." She grabbed my arm and guided me toward the snack stand. I started to resist, then glanced over at Kevin Reynolds and changed my mind.

"Okay, I'm coming," I said, watching him out of the corner of my eye.

We bought our drinks, and I started to sit down at the table nearest the snack stand. Alice headed for another one, closer to the boys.

"Alice!" I whispered. She just kept going. I swallowed hard and followed her to a table perhaps twenty feet away from Kevin Reynolds and his friends.

"Try to keep your voice down," said Alice as we took our seats. "And whatever you do, don't look at him."

15

"This is crazy."

"Ssh! I'm trying to hear what they're saying."

Just then a woman with a stroller sat down at a table near us, and the baby started to cry.

"Oh, great," said Alice. She scooted her chair away from the baby and toward Kevin's table. "I can't hear a thing. How about you? You're closer."

"I'm just sipping my drink, minding my own business."

The baby stopped crying for a second, and I heard Kevin's voice. I couldn't understand what he was saying, but I did make out the word *girl*. I leaned back in my chair, hoping to catch the rest. There was a terrible sinking feeling in the pit of my stomach as I felt the chair balance for a moment on the two back legs, then slowly move past the point of no return.

"Becky, you've got a funny look on your face," said Alice.

"Whoaooaargh," I replied.

I kicked my legs and pinwheeled my arms. There was a crash, and the next thing I knew, I was sprawled on the linoleum floor with my legs in the air and a large Coke resting upside down on the lap of my jeans.

I suppose I should have been grateful not to have hit my head on the floor, but that's not what I was worried about. I pushed the hair back from my eyes and stole a glance at Kevin Reynolds, praying that somehow he hadn't noticed.

He and his entire group rose to give me a standing ovation, complete with whistles and stomps and whoops of approval.

Then Alice was beside me. "Becky, are you okay?"

"I'm dying a slow, painful death," I said. "Other than that, I'm fine."

We decided to leave, since I didn't feel like spending the afternoon explaining to people why my pants were soaked.

"You're pretty quiet," said Alice as we walked home.

"I'm thinking of joining a monastery," I said.

"I don't think they take girls."

"Okay then, the circus. I'd make a great clown."

"I'm sorry, Becky. It was my fault for dragging you over to the food park."

"That's true."

"Hey," she protested, "you're not supposed to say that."

"Okay, it was ninety percent your fault. The other ten was mine for agreeing to go."

"That's better. I guess."

"You know," I said, "you can make it up to me."

"How?"

"Do whatever I ask for the next twenty-five years." I pointed at a shop across the street. "For starters, I'll take a frozen yogurt with everything on it."

By Monday I was back in school and feeling better. I'd been relieved to see that my mishap hadn't made the evening news. No one on the street had burst out laughing when they saw me. And I found that no matter how famous I might have become at Brentwood Prep, the kids at Sunnyslope Elementary were less interested in me than in what the cafeteria was serving for lunch.

As a matter of fact, it happened to be frankfurters and beans. Alice, sitting beside me, took one look at her plate and pushed it away.

"I'm sorry," she said, "but I don't eat anything with the word *furter* in it."

"The stuff's really not so bad," I said, trying a bite. "Anyway, I heard the preservatives are good for your complexion."

"I'd rather look at boys."

I did a quick check of the vicinity and was pleased to see that none of the boys was over five and a half feet tall or wore a letterman's jacket. This was a group I could deal with.

"I can't believe the way Darryl Cunningham rolls up the cuffs on his pants," said Alice. "What is he, a lumberjack? And look at Kenny Singleton. Somebody should tell him you don't wear purple and yellow unless you're the Easter Bunny."

"I like Kenny Singleton. He's sweet."

"The kid's warped. I heard he sleeps with Big Bird."

"Look," I said, "there's Matt Yaslavsky. He's got a great smile, doesn't he?"

"Sure, if you like the glint of metal."

"Plenty of kids have braces, including you."

"My point exactly. Besides, when they tighten them, it affects your brain. I speak from personal experience."

"Alice," I said, "you do this all the time. You say you're going to watch boys, then you manage to find something wrong with all of them."

"Not all. Just the ones in elementary school."

"I hate to break the news, Alice, but you and I aren't exactly doing postgraduate work."

She sighed and shook her head. "Becky, Becky, Becky. Let me explain something to you. In every kid's life there

18

comes a time when the hormones kick in and the body starts changing shape.''

"I know all about that stuff. I'm a living example.''

"The changes happen around the fifth grade, right? Okay, the third grade in your case.''

"Right,'' I said.

"Wrong! Or at least half wrong. Sure, girls change in the fifth grade, but for boys it doesn't happen until the seventh grade or so. In other words, there's a critical two-year gap in which girls are women and boys are shrimps.''

"Thank you, Dr. Biddle.''

"The sex gap, I call it.''

"You mean there isn't one boy in the whole sixth grade that you like?''

She thought about it for a minute. "Okay, Philip Krasner's kind of cute.''

"I thought you didn't like shrimps.''

"There are exceptions to every rule. His father owns a steel company.''

I took another bite of my frankfurters and beans, and Alice continued to scan the area for boys.

"Get a load of this,'' she said. "Some kid's wearing a coat and tie.''

I looked up, and sure enough, across the cafeteria was a boy with a blue pinstripe suit. He was barely four feet tall, with dark hair, rosy cheeks, and a cocky grin.

"Hey,'' snorted Alice, "he's got on tennis shoes. And check out his friend.''

The boy in the suit was standing with his arms crossed, looking around the place as if he owned it. Every once in a while he would get a funny, secret look on his face and say something out of the corner of his mouth, like a gangster in an old movie. His friend, a skinny kid with a caved-in chest, would nod excitedly and write in his notebook.

"I wonder what they're doing," I said.

The boy turned toward us, and his eyes got kind of wide.

"I don't know," said Alice with a smirk, "but right now they're looking straight at you."

3

# THE EYE

 Sammy

It's a few days after the phone call to Janie Hodges. Gus and I are scoping out the cafeteria as part of my survey of women.

"My stomach hurts," whines Gus. "I think I ate too fast."

"You're just mad because you couldn't build a fort out of frankfurter skin," I tell him. "Besides, the reason we ate fast was so we could start the survey."

"Why couldn't we wait until later?"

"Gus," I explain patiently, "the cafeteria's a perfect place for checking out a woman. You can tell a lot by the way she eats. Little things people don't usually notice. For instance, does she yell at her friends with her mouth full? Does she tear up her napkin to make spit wads? Does she have a milk mustache?"

I point to a table nearby. "Take Roxie Lundquist. Ever notice the way she shapes her bread into little squares to form dice?"

"Hey, how does she do that?" asks Gus.

"Or Irene Klump. See anything funny about her?"

21

Gus squints over in her direction. "Her hair?"

"No, I mean the way she eats."

"But she's not eating," he tells me. "There's no food on her plate."

"Exactly, because she already wolfed it down. Now I ask you, what kind of person finishes lunch in three minutes flat?"

"We did."

"I'm talking about women."

"Maybe she's doing a survey on men," says Gus.

I look to see if he's joking. He's not. "I can see we're starting at a pretty basic level," I tell him. "I'm going to give you some background information about women. You might want to take notes."

"Huh? Oh, right." Gus whips out his notebook and one of those mechanical pencils that write in four colors. "Which color do you think I should use?"

I just stare at him.

"Maybe red," he says. "It's kind of like lipstick. But my sister likes green. Of course, most people think blue is nicer. But black's easier to read."

"Gus. Are you finished?"

"Red, definitely red."

"Try to concentrate," I say.

"Hey, this thing is jammed," says Gus. He's fiddling with the pen, pounding on the top of it with his palm. I calmly take it away from him, click it so the red point comes out, and hand it back.

"First off," I say, "women tend to cry a lot."

". . . cry . . . a . . . lot," says Gus, printing every word

22

carefully in his notebook. He shows me the page. "Is that okay, Sammy?"

"Fine, fine," I tell him. "Most of the time, all they think about is mushy, romantic stuff. They do things like write letters to Mel Gibson and memorize the words of their favorite love song."

I start pacing back and forth. It gets the ideas flowing. I can feel the brain waves zipping back and forth inside my head. "Women are always going on diets. But they have this uncontrollable urge to bake chocolate chip cookies. It's one of the mysteries of modern science."

Gus nods and keeps writing. He sticks his tongue out of the side of his mouth, the way he does during spelling tests.

"They go around in groups," I tell him, "so they've got somebody to listen when they think of things to say. Which is all the time. When they're not together, they use the phone."

Gus is really into it now, clicking his pen and scribbling like mad in his notebook.

"Basically, they're weak," I say. "And they're looking for somebody strong. That's where the two of us come in."

I glance over at Gus. "Okay, got that so far?" I ask.

"Right, Sammy," he says. But I notice there's a funny look on his face.

I check his notebook. At the top he's scrawled a few words. Underneath that is a picture of a rocket ship taking off into space. The ship is black, the earth is green, the sky is blue, and the rocket flames are red.

"This pen is great for rocket ships," says Gus.

I shake my head. "Let's try a new topic, huh?"

"Should I still take notes?"

"Yeah, but you might want to start a new page. We're going to call this 'Tips for Impressing Women.' "

"Right," says Gus. He bends over his notebook again. For all I know, he's drawing a picture of Donald Duck.

"Okay, number one," I say. "Never carry an umbrella. It's a sign of weakness."

"Wow, I never knew that."

"Number two. Always use an after-shave, even if you don't shave."

Gus sniffs in my direction. "So that's what that smell is."

"Number three. Never say 'I don't know.' "

"What if you don't know?"

"Pretend you do," I tell him. "Number four. Talk in a low, soft voice. This is called the voice of love. Women go nuts over it."

"What does it sound like?"

"I'll do it for you later. I don't want any women bothering me right now. Number five, and this is the most important one of all. Dare to be different."

"You mean wear a suit like you do?"

"Gus, that wouldn't be different. That would be the same."

"Then how do I know what to do?" he asks.

"It's up to you. That's the whole point." I clap him on the shoulder. "Relax. You can think of something later. In the meantime, we have a survey to do."

We wander around the cafeteria, looking at different women. I tell Gus to write down anything about them that might be important, such as stuff that would drive you crazy.

For instance, Marsha Brennaman looks fine but has a habit of picking her ear with a paper clip. Debbie Waters seems great until she laughs, and then she snorts like a pig.

Of course, we're careful not to be too obvious. When I spot a woman, I don't point or anything like that. I just kind of tilt my head in her direction so Gus can see who I'm looking at. When I tell him something, I talk out of the corner of my mouth.

As we get to the back of the cafeteria, I see two women I don't recognize. I figure they must be new. One of them has brownish hair and freckles and is almost as skinny as Gus. But she's not the one I'm looking at. It's her friend I'm interested in.

She's the most gorgeous woman I've ever seen.

She looks fourteen or fifteen at least, even though I know she could only be in the sixth grade. She's tall, with all the equipment to match, so at first I think maybe she flunked a grade or two. Then I look at her eyes, which shine like a couple of blue spotlights, and I know she's too smart for that. Her hair is gold and curls down over her shoulders. She's got on a white blouse and green skirt that look kind of plain, but there's something classy about the way she wears them. While I watch, she pushes her hair back behind one ear and smiles. Suddenly the whole area brightens up, like when you clean off your car windshield with one of those rubber squeegees. I could stand there forever and just look at her. The only problem is, she's looking at me.

I reach over and grab Gus's notebook and pen. I look up at the ceiling and start pointing to it and pretending to talk to Gus.

"What are you doing?" he says.

25

"Just nod and smile," I tell him out of the corner of my mouth.

I start to jot down something in the notebook as part of my act, but there's a huge red, blue, green, and black dragon covering the whole page. I stick the end of the pen in my mouth and study the dragon like it's some kind of special report on the building.

"Hey, don't chew on my pen," Gus says. "You might have germs."

"Yes, of course, I see," I tell Gus in a loud voice.

"You see what?" he asks.

I close the notebook, grab Gus by his scrawny arm, and lead him off. When we're a safe distance away, I look back at the woman. She's talking to her friend. Thanks to some quick thinking on my part, she probably figures we're student architects or something.

Suddenly I feel great. "Come on," I say, "let's go get a candy bar."

"What about the survey?" asks Gus.

"It's finished."

That afternoon I quietly ask around and find out some key facts about the woman. It turns out her name is Becky Davidson and she's in Mr. Lawrence's sixth-grade class. She's smart and she loves to read. She works in the library after school a couple of days a week, along with her skinny friend Alice Biddle.

"Perfect," I say to Gus after the three o'clock bell.

"How can you say that? I flunked the arithmetic test."

"Gus, I'm talking about women, not a few lousy math problems. Okay, we've planned our strategy and identified our target."

"You mean that great big girl? What if she decides to beat us up?"

"Get ahold of yourself, Gus. Now, the next step is to set up a meeting, but to make sure it seems accidental. The whole idea is to have her notice you before you supposedly notice her. Then, when you see she's watching, you give her the Eye."

"The Eye?"

"It's a way of looking at a woman to show how sensitive and sincere you are."

"Wow," he says, "do you think I could do it?"

"You'd better just watch me this time," I tell him.

We walk into the library. Just like I was hoping, there's Becky Davidson. She and her friend have one of those metal carts and are putting books back on the shelf.

I position myself down the aisle, where I take a book off the shelf and thumb through it. Gus does the same thing a few feet away, only he hasn't noticed that his book is upside down. I want to say something to him but decide not to risk it.

I notice that Becky Davidson and her friend are whispering. I can't hear what they're saying, but they seem all giggly and excited. Good sign. I check out of the corner of my eye and see that they're looking in my direction. I decide this is the moment. I toss Gus a wink, then turn toward Becky Davidson and give her the Eye.

I've seen Nick do it a million times, so it's almost like second nature to me. I kind of smile, but only with one side of my mouth. I let my eyelids droop, like I'm sleepy or something. Also, I flare my nostrils.

27

I can tell it's having an effect because her eyes open wide and she stops giggling. She just stares at me for a long time.

"Are you all right?" she says.

"Never felt better," I tell her.

"You looked like you were going to pass out for a minute there."

A sense of humor—I love it. Figuring I'm on a roll, I say, "I'm looking for a book. You may have heard of it. I think it's about war and peace."

"You mean *War and Peace?*"

"Right. Do you know the name of it?"

"That *is* the name of it," she says. "It's by Tolstoy."

I shake my head. "Must be another book. This one had a snappier title. When you read as many books as I do, it's hard to keep track of them all."

"Oh, really?" says her skinny friend Alice, who's standing right behind her. "What's the last one you read?"

I desperately try to remember the name of any book in the world. "Let's see," I say finally, "I think it was *Lifestyles of the Rich and Famous.*"

"That's a great book, all right," says Alice. "I liked it almost as much as 'General Hospital.' "

"Yeah, that one was good, too," I say. I turn back to Becky. "By the way, I'm Sammy Carducci."

"I'm Becky Davidson," she says. "This is my friend Alice Biddle."

I shake Alice's hand, which catches her by surprise. Then I do something that amazes even me. When Becky holds out her hand, I kiss it, like I'm a knight in some King Arthur movie.

28

I'm not sure why I did it. It's not something I planned. But I do know that it feels good. Her skin is soft and warm, and I get a whiff of something that smells like flowers. I look up at her and see that her cheeks have turned pink.

"Ooh, gross," says Alice. "Here's my handkerchief, Becky."

"That's okay," says Becky, smiling. Obviously, she's fallen for the old Carducci charm.

Feeling good, I put my hands in my pockets and casually lean back against the nearest object. Unfortunately, it's the book cart. I feel it start to roll backward. I try to get my hands free, but it's too late. Books go flying everywhere, and I hit the floor with a thud. Gus appears at my side to help me up. I brush him off and pop right back up.

"No problem, no problem," I say.

"Is this guy a friend of yours?" Alice asks me, looking at Gus suspiciously.

I tug at my lapels. "Hey, what do you know, it's my buddy Gus. I guess he just happened to be nearby reading a book."

"He reads upside down?" she says.

I hear a noise and glance up to see Mrs. Stanford, the librarian. She usually smiles a lot, but today she looks kind of sad. Shaking her head, she says, "Girls, I'm disappointed in you."

"It wasn't our fault," says Alice. "These two creeps were bothering us."

Becky starts to say something, but I speak up first. "Alice is right, Mrs. Stanford. It was our fault. Totally."

"It was?" says Gus. "Oh, yeah, it was."

Mrs. Stanford looks back and forth at Gus and me. "Maybe you two boys should go on home. Remember, these girls have a job to do."

As we go out the door, I glance over my shoulder and see that Becky Davidson is looking at me. Our eyes meet for a second. Then I turn and follow Gus into the hall.

# THE QUESTION

✎ Becky

"Just once I wish we could have pastrami. Or beef curry, or shish kebab, or blackened swordfish. Or blackened anything, for that matter. Everything on this table is so *white*."

I was sitting at dinner with my parents on a Monday night, gazing at the parched chicken breast on my plate.

"There's some spray paint in the garage," my mom said, spooning gravy over her mashed potatoes.

"You know what I mean. It seems like we have broiled chicken every Monday night."

"We do," she said, smiling.

"I like broiled chicken," said my dad. "On Monday afternoons I can't wait to get home and sink my fork into it."

"That's sweet, dear. Isn't he nice, Becky?"

"We're all nice. Sometimes it makes me want to scream."

"Go ahead," she said, "but please show a little consideration and do it in the next room."

"Every Tuesday we have fish," my dad recited happily. "Every Wednesday is tuna casserole. Thursdays are pot

31

roast. And on Fridays we get wild and crazy. Either hot dogs or hamburgers—our choice!''

I sighed.

My mom and dad had never been rich, so for most of my life we'd lived in an apartment downtown. Finally this past summer they'd saved up enough money to buy a home in a new development outside the city, and we'd moved to a land of freshly seeded lawns, tiny trees, and rows of identical houses. For my parents it was a dream come true. My mom became an avid gardener, and my dad took up puttering. Any time of night or day I'd see him wandering the halls, a dazed grin on his face, carrying things like socket wrenches and needle-nose pliers.

"What are you doing, Dad?" I'd ask him.

"Oh, just puttering around the house," he'd say.

I never knew where he was going or where he'd been— I'm not sure he did, either—but I could tell he was happy. So was my mom. She subscribed to all the usual home magazines, plus a few I'd never heard of: *Molding Monthly, Closet Beautiful, You and Your Faucets.* Her latest thing was menu planning, based on the days of the week.

"You know," I said, salting the chicken, "sometimes I miss our apartment."

"Yeah, this place has too much room," said my dad.

My mom nodded. "I miss hearing the neighbors fight."

"I know it wasn't perfect," I said. "But I liked being able to walk outside anytime and find people doing things. Maybe there was a policeman directing traffic or a kid skateboarding or old Mr. Thomas selling newspapers. Maybe I'd walk down a few doors and buy a candy bar.

Maybe I'd just sit on our steps and watch the cars hit potholes in the street."

"I'm sure we could arrange to get some potholes here," said my mom.

"There were different kinds of people in the neighborhood, too. They didn't all have lawn mowers and minivans. Some of them didn't even have kids."

"Shocking," she said.

"There ought to be a law," said my dad.

I shook my head. "You guys are impossible."

My mom reached over and gently put her hand on mine. "Come on, honey. What do you expect from Mr. and Mrs. Suburbia?"

It was a nickname they'd given themselves when we bought the house, and it always made me smile. "I guess I don't really mind living here, Mom. And I do like my school."

"How's Alice?" asked my dad.

"Still looking for boys."

He chuckled. "What's she going to do when she finds one?"

"I don't think it'll happen for a while. She's got her standards, you know."

"What about you?" he asked.

"I've got standards, too."

"I mean, how are you feeling about boys these days?"

"In general? Fine, I guess."

"Is there anybody in particular that you like?" asked my mom.

I noticed my dad paying close attention. He'd been nervous about this topic ever since I'd developed my first curves.

"Well, there is this one boy," I said. "I don't know if you could say I actually like him. He's kind of strange."

"Oh, great," said my dad.

"For instance, he wears a suit."

"You mean like a jogging suit?"

"A suit suit, with a tie. Oh, and sneakers."

"Naturally," my mom said.

"He's about four feet tall, and he's got a skinny friend who follows him around taking notes."

My dad gave me a funny look. "Of all the boys at school, this is the one you picked?"

"I didn't pick him. I barely know him. I just think he's interesting."

"Does he have a name?" said my mom.

"Sammy Carducci."

"How did you meet?" she asked.

"He was staring at me in the library today. You should have seen the expression on his face. I thought he was going to throw up. Then he introduced himself and fell over the book cart."

"Sounds like a great kid," my dad said.

"Ralph, please."

"Mrs. Stanford caught Alice and me talking to him, but he took the blame."

"That was nice," said my mom.

"He even kissed my hand," I said. "It was weird. But there was something sweet about it."

My dad raised his eyebrows.

"Okay, he's different," I said. "He probably doesn't eat

broiled chicken on Monday nights. Maybe that's why I think he's interesting." I looked down at my mashed potatoes. "I don't even know why I'm talking about this."

I was quiet for the rest of the meal, while my mom and dad discussed their latest home projects. Later, I cleared the table and my mom served ice cream for dessert.

It was vanilla.

"Tetherball," snorted Alice. "You stand next to this pole, and there's this ball tied onto it with a rope, and you hit the ball with your fist. What kind of sport is that?"

It was a couple of days later, and Alice and I were at recess, which for us meant sitting on a bench, watching the other kids play tetherball. Alice had very strong feelings on the subject.

"Most of the time," she went on, "you miss the ball. But then if you do hit it, you practically break your hand. Meanwhile, every time you raise your arm above your head, some boy's trying to look up your skirt."

"At least it's exercise," I pointed out.

"What is it they say? 'Horses sweat, men perspire, women glow'? Well, I've got news for them. When I exercise, I sweat. You want me to play tetherball? Fine. Just don't ask me to go back to class afterward."

"Excuse me," said a small voice behind us. We turned around and saw a third-grade boy holding a crumpled pink slip toward Alice. "Are you Alice Biddle?"

"That's right."

"I'm supposed to give you this." He handed her the paper and scuttled off.

Alice unfolded the note. "It's a summons to the nurse's

35

office. Something about dental plaque. And listen to this: 'Please do not bring any friends.' "

I glanced at the slip. "The nurse's handwriting sure isn't very neat. Look at all the fingerprints on this thing."

"Well, if she wants to look inside my mouth, she'll have to wash her hands first." Alice got up and smoothed her skirt. "I guess I'll see you in class."

When she was gone, I sat back on the bench, enjoying the warm breeze and sunshine. A few minutes later, Sammy Carducci came along, wearing his usual suit and sneakers. He was walking by himself with his hands in his pockets, whistling and making a show of looking in the other direction. In fact, his body was turned so far that he was almost walking sideways, like a crab. As he drew near, he turned and saw me.

"Let's see," he said, with one hand on his chin and the other pointing at me, "it's, uh, Becky, am I right?"

"Hi, Sammy," I said.

"I don't believe this coincidence. We meet on Monday, and whammo, I run across you two days later on the playground."

"Yeah, it's pretty amazing, all right."

"Hey, you wouldn't mind if I sat down next to you there, would you?"

"Be my guest."

He chuckled. " 'Be my guest.' I like that." He unbuttoned his jacket and slid onto the bench next to me. Or at least he tried to slide, but the bench was a little tall and he ended up having to kind of hop up onto it. Once he was seated, his feet dangled an inch or two above the ground.

36

He reached inside his jacket, pulled out a pack of gum, and offered me a stick.

"Juicy Fruit," he said. "Only the best."

"No, thanks."

He plucked a stick from the pack, unwrapped it, and folded it into his mouth. "Keeps me relaxed," he said.

I had to turn away to hide my smile. If this was relaxed, I'd hate to see him when he was tense. His eyes shifted around, his eyebrows wiggled like caterpillars, and a grin was pasted across his face that looked like something from a horror movie.

"You know, Becky, did I ever tell you how terrific you are?"

"Well, no," I said. "We just met two days ago."

"Huh? Oh, yeah. Right." He thought for a minute, then said, "The first time I saw you, there was this incredible rush."

"You mean like a noise of some kind?"

"No, just this incredible, I don't know, rush. You know, like a rush. I think it might have been a vibe or something."

"Good vibes? Is that what you're talking about?"

"Yeah, that's it. I can't believe how you knew exactly what I meant. That's incredible. In fact, I'm getting another rush just thinking about it."

"Where's your friend Gus?" I asked.

"Uh, playing kickball, I think."

As a matter of fact, I'd just spotted Gus peeking at us from behind a tree. "Hey, there he is. Hi, Gus!" I called, waving.

37

Sammy, thinking my attention was diverted, glared at the tree and made a quick motion with his hand. Gus ducked out of sight. Then Sammy turned back to me, shaking his head.

"Nah, must have been somebody else," he said.

There was a long silence after that. Sammy peered out across the playground, anxiously tugging at his tie and picking lint off his pants.

"Here comes Alice," I said. "That's funny; she looks upset."

Sammy whirled toward me and in a strange voice bleated, "Wannagotothedance?"

"Pardon me?"

He cleared his throat. "The dance. Wanna go? With me? To the dance?"

"Sammy, how nice," I said.

He kept glancing over toward Alice. The closer she got, the more agitated he became. Finally he croaked, "I better leave."

"Don't you want me to answer your question?"

"Uh, yeah, okay." Alice was close now. Sammy's head swiveled back and forth between us like a high-speed windshield wiper.

"You seem a little nervous," I said.

He tried to laugh nonchalantly, but it was more of a cackle. "Me, nervous? You gotta be kidding."

Alice approached, her eyes flashing. "What happened?" I asked.

"I just made a complete fool of myself, that's all. I walked into the nurse's office and told her I was there to have my dental plaque checked. She asked me if I thought

38

I had a problem with plaque, which made it sound like my whole mouth was coated with the stuff. I said, 'No, but apparently you thought I did.' I showed her the summons, and she said somebody must be playing a trick on me because the note was forged. Just about that time, a teacher came out from the back of the office, where he must have been standing the whole time. You know who it was? Mr. Lawrence! I've never been so humiliated in my entire life. He probably thinks my mouth is all diseased and I need dental surgery."

She clutched the summons in her hand and looked around the playground. "Where's that little kid who brought me this? I'm going to wring his neck."

When Alice said the word *neck,* Sammy tugged at his collar, and all at once I knew who'd written the note. The third grader was innocent, of course. The real forger was someone who had wanted to get me alone for a few minutes. He'd succeeded but hadn't allowed himself quite enough time.

Suddenly the expression on Sammy's face changed. You could almost see a light bulb go on over his head. "Excuse me, miss," he said to Alice, "I don't know if you remember me."

"You're the guy from the library," she said.

"Sammy Carducci's the name. I was just talking to Miss Davidson here and couldn't help but overhear what you were saying."

"If you breathe a word of this plaque stuff to anybody," said Alice, "I'll cut off your tie and stuff it up your nose."

Sammy winced. "Actually, I thought I could help. Maybe I could make a few discreet inquiries and find out who did it. Once I knew, I'd use some subtle persuasion, if you know what I mean, to make sure it never, ever happened again. Guaranteed."

Alice eyed him suspiciously. "What's in it for you?"

"The satisfaction of a job well done."

"Let him do it, Alice," I said. Sammy looked at me, surprised. I looked right back. "I have a feeling it might be easy for him to find this person."

His face turned pale. As he stared at me, Alice thought it over. She usually took my advice pretty seriously. Finally she shrugged. "Well, okay. But I'm sure going to miss squeezing somebody's neck and watching their eyes bug out."

"You won't regret this," said Sammy. "In fact, I'm going to get started on it right now."

As he turned to leave, I said, "Sammy, I just wanted to mention one thing before you go."

"What's that?"

"The answer is yes."

# THE DANCE

✏ Sammy

"WHAT'S YOUR SECRET, Nickie?" I ask my brother.

He's driving me over to Becky's house to pick her up for the dance. I figure as long as I've got his undivided attention, I might as well get a few tips on women.

He laughs. "What do you care, Sammy? You're just a kid."

"Hey, I'm going on a date, aren't I? And I ask you, is this a kid's outfit?" I happen to be wearing a spiffy tuxedo. I pull out a pair of shades and casually slip them on.

He grins and shakes his head. "You're something else, you know it?"

"So tell me the secret, Nickie. Give it to me straight."

He runs his fingers through his hair. I check out the way he does it and make a note to practice in front of the mirror.

"Okay, there's a lot of things," he says. "You dress sharp. You talk civilized, which means never swearing. You tell women how good they look, even if they don't. But the most important thing is, they've got to know who's boss. Now, they'll throw you a little test every once in a while, like nagging or begging you for this or that. You've got to

41

nip that in the bud. Sometimes you've got to be firm. Tell them what you want, and let them know you mean it."

"Is that what you do with Cindy?" I ask. He's been seeing a lot of her since the phone call.

"That's what I do with all of them."

When we turn onto Becky's street, I check my pocket to make sure I have the address. We're going to need it because it's the craziest street I've ever seen. All the houses look alike. They're sort of a light brown color with the same roof and door and windows. In front of all of them there's a dwarf tree with a few tiny branches.

We find Becky's number and pull into the driveway. Nick waits in the car while I walk up the front steps and knock. When the door opens, I'm standing face-to-face with a vision of beauty, by which I mean Becky Davidson.

She's got on this long dress that looks like something you'd see in a magazine. It's a shiny white color, almost like it glows. It comes up to her neck, where she's wearing some light blue beads. Her hair is piled on top of her head, and there's a blue ribbon holding it together. Her cheeks are pink. So are her lips. She looks incredible.

"Come on in, Sammy," she says.

I float inside like I'm on a cloud. Behind Becky there's a man and a woman who I figure are her parents. Her mother has the same smile as Becky. Her dad seems kind of nervous. He's staring at me like I'm a creature from Mars.

"Sammy Carducci?" he says.

I nod. "You must be Mr. Davidson." I hold out my hand, and he leans down and shakes it. I turn to Mrs. Davidson. "And this must be your lovely bride."

42

Something about that seems funny to her, which is fine. I like people to be happy.

"Do you want to come sit down for a minute, Sammy?" she says as we shake hands.

"Gee, Mrs. Davidson, that sounds swell, but my brother's waiting out in the car."

"Maybe we should get going, Mom," says Becky.

"Oh, I almost forgot, Becky," I say. "I brought something for you." I pull a box from behind my back and open it up. It's a corsage, which is a special kind of flower that girls wear at dances.

"Sammy, it's beautiful," says Becky. "You didn't have to do this."

"Yes, I did. My brother said so. He knows all about this stuff." I take the corsage out of the box. "He told me I'm supposed to pin it on your dress."

I try, but it's hard to see very much because I'm still wearing my shades. Plus Becky's so tall that I'm having trouble looking up that high. For a minute I think of pinning the corsage down by her waist, where everything's in full view, but then I decide that would look dumb. Next I start worrying that no matter where I put it, I might accidentally stick her with the pin. I kind of circle around the front of Becky, trying to decide what to do.

Mrs. Davidson, who's got her hand over her mouth, coughs and says, "Would you like me to do it for you?"

"Maybe so," I tell her. "I don't want to injure your daughter."

She pins the corsage up by Becky's shoulder and we talk for a few minutes; then Becky and I head for the car. When Nick sees us coming, he stares at Becky. I can tell he's

43

impressed. I guess he figured she'd be some mousy little kid with pigtails. He figured wrong.

I open the back door and we climb in. I introduce Nick as our chauffeur. I get a big laugh out of that one, but Nick doesn't think it's so funny. As we drive to school, Nick keeps looking at Becky in the rearview mirror. Meanwhile, I keep her entertained with some of my typical charming conversation. I feel like a king, only my throne is the back seat of Nick's Grand Am.

"Thank you, James," I tell Nick when we pull into the school parking lot. "We won't be needing the car for the next few hours."

"Lucky thing," he says, "because it's not available. I'll be back at ten."

As we get out, I consider slipping him a fiver but decide not to. Instead, I give him a thumbs-up. He burns rubber out of the parking lot.

When we walk into the school gym, I can hardly believe it's the same place where Mr. Hoolihan tries to teach us wrestling. There's crepe paper hanging everyplace, and balloons are tied to the basketball rims. There's a sign saying WELCOME, SIXTH GRADERS! At the front of the gym is a cassette deck with a couple of big speakers, and some geeky kid is fiddling with the dials. I can tell he's a member of the audiovisual squad.

There's music playing, but no one is dancing. The girls are standing against one wall, and the boys are over against the other one. They're huddled together in groups, trying to look cool. Every few seconds they look toward the other wall, then go back to talking. Everybody's all dressed up for the occasion. Even Bubba Branley and Lois Friedman,

44

the two grungiest kids in Mrs. McNulty's class, look like they took a bath.

I spot Gus with the boys. I kind of nod to him but just keep walking. Becky sees her friend Alice and waves. I look around for a place where we can talk and notice ten or so people who are actually on dates like Becky and me. We decide to go stand with them. On the way over, people seem to stop what they're doing and stare at us.

"Check it out," I whisper to Becky. "They can't believe how great we look."

For some reason, she laughs. It's a terrific laugh, not high and piercing at all. She takes my arm and kind of pats it as we walk.

"Isn't this exciting?" she says.

"Yeah, I guess it sort of is."

"I'm glad you asked me to come with you, Sammy."

"No problem," I tell her.

As we cross the floor, there's a loud clunk and a whine on the PA system, and Mrs. McNulty's voice comes on.

"Attention, please," she says in that singsongy voice of hers. "We're now serving punch and cookies at the front table."

The place goes nuts. Everybody who was trying to figure out what to do with themselves charges the table and begins stuffing their face. In other words, the whole sixth grade. They might not know how to dance, but they can sure eat.

Becky looks at me and shrugs. "I guess we might as well go over there."

"Sure," I say. "I'll treat you to a cookie."

When we get in line, Alice is right behind us. She starts talking to Becky but ignores me. Fine. The two of them drift a little ways away, and just about that time Gus walks up to me. He's wearing one of those clip-on bow ties and a sport coat that comes halfway down to his knees.

"Wow, you look great!" he says.

"You look all right yourself."

I wink at him and jerk my head over in Alice's direction, hoping he'll catch my drift. He just grins. I do it again.

"Is something wrong with your neck?" he asks me.

"Fine, fine," I say out loud. Then I whisper, "What are you waiting for? Here's your chance to practice your moves with women. Look who's over there."

"Becky? I thought she was with you," Gus whispers.

"I'm talking about her friend Alice."

"She hates me," says Gus. "When we were in the library, she called me a creep."

"Women are always saying things like that. Usually it means they like you."

"Really?"

"This is your big chance, Gus."

He takes a deep breath, then starts to edge over toward Alice. Every once in a while he glances back to see whether he's doing okay, and I nod. Finally he plants himself a few feet away from her.

He gives her the Eye.

Alice doesn't notice at first and just keeps chattering away to Becky. Then she spots Gus. She tries to ignore him but finally sees he's not going to stop.

So she gives him the Eye right back.

Actually, it's not the Eye. It's more like a high-powered laser beam that destroys everything in its path. Gus throws me a panicked look. I decide it's time to step in.

46

I move over to where Becky and Alice are talking. "So, how's it going?"

"Call off your friend, Carducci," says Alice.

"It's okay, Alice," says Becky.

I position Gus so he's standing next to Alice. The right side of his face is twitching, and I notice one end of his clip-on bow tie has come loose, so the tie is dangling down the front of his shirt. I reach over and clip it back in place.

"I don't think you two have officially met," I say. "Gus Gaffney, this is the lovely Miss Alice Biddle."

"Give me a break," says Alice. Gus throws her a sickly smile.

Just then the line moves, and it's our turn in front of the refreshment table. While Gus, Alice, and Becky grab cookies, I hand them paper cups full of punch. I hold my cup in the air.

"I'd like to propose a toast," I say. "To Becky Davidson, the most beautiful woman in the whole sixth grade."

Becky grins. Alice rolls her eyes. Alice, Gus, and I touch our cups together and take a gulp of punch.

"And here's another toast," I say. "To Sunnyslope Elementary and all the teachers, librarians, playground monitors, crossing guards, janitors, PTA members—"

"Keep the line moving!" somebody calls out behind us.

"Hey, do you mind?" I shout back.

"Maybe we should move on," says Becky.

I decide to forget the toast, since I'm not sure where I was going with it anyway. The four of us find a spot near the end of the table and munch on our cookies for a few minutes. Nobody says much.

"Look," says Becky when she finishes her punch, "some people are dancing."

Sure enough, there's a group in the middle of the floor, bouncing around in time to the music.

"Want to go out there?" I ask her.

She nods, and I offer her my arm. For the next ten minutes we give a textbook demonstration of fast dancing. Becky looks sensational. I try out a couple of new moves I've been practicing in front of the mirror. Then the music slows down, and I step in close the way Nick showed me. But the closer I get, the more I can see that I've got a problem.

I'm shorter than Becky, which means my eyes aren't quite even with her eyes. They're not even with her chin, either. You might say they fall a little bit lower.

For a while I glance to one side or the other, but that doesn't work too well. Then I try staring at the floor. The top of my head bumps against her and I jump back. Finally I look right up into her face, which seems okay because she's smiling at me. I smile back, but after a few minutes my neck starts to ache. By the time the song ends, I feel like I've been sitting in the front row of the movies.

The rest of the night goes by so fast I can hardly believe it. We eat some cookies. We watch Gus try to give Alice the Eye a few more times. Becky and I talk to Mr. Lawrence, and she manages to get through the conversation without giggling once. We check out a rumor that Sissy Krenman and Wayne Hotchkiss were seen making out behind the stairs, which turns out to be Sissy Krenman and *Clara* Hotchkiss, Wayne's sister, playing Crazy Eights.

Then, first thing you know, Mrs. McNulty starts flashing the lights to let everybody know the dance is over.

"I had fun," says Becky when I drop her off at her doorstep.

"Me, too," I tell her.

She pulls the key from her purse and unlocks the door, then takes a step inside. She stops for a second, and before I know what's hit me, she leans down and gives me a peck on the cheek. Then she's gone.

Who needs Nick to drive me home? I can fly.

# THE **H**UNK

✐ Becky

Aɪɪᴄᴇ ɢʀᴏᴀɴᴇᴅ. "Oh no, not Captain Bob again."

It was Monday after the dance, and Alice and I had just entered the school auditorium with Mr. Lawrence's class for a special assembly. Standing at the front of the auditorium was a gaunt, white-haired man wearing a fireman's uniform and a vacant smile.

It was the dreaded Captain Bob.

When I'd first arrived at Sunnyslope Elementary, some of the other kids had told me about him. He'd been coming to the school as long as anyone could remember, and every year he did the same thing. He would show a film about fire prevention that must have been made when they first invented flames; then he'd pull out a beat-up chart with diagrams and talk to the students about fireproofing their homes. He always addressed his listeners as if they were two-year-olds, which didn't make him the most popular speaker of the year. At the end of the program, he'd describe the Junior Fire Chief Club. He'd pass out cheap cardboard badges and make everyone stand and recite the Junior Fire Chief pledge until they could say it by heart.

Alice and I took seats as close to Mr. Lawrence as possible, so we'd at least have something interesting to look at. Shortly after that, Captain Bob launched into his routine. I noticed Mr. Farnsworth, the school principal, standing off to the side, beaming. For some reason, he thought Captain Bob was wonderful. There were rumors that he and the captain were related, maybe even brothers. I doubted it, but I had to admit they had that same goofy smile.

In our section nobody was paying much attention. Shelley Robinson was braiding Dianne Yablonski's hair. Davey Dobbs was holding a pencil in front of his face and looking at it cross-eyed. The Scarlatti twins had devised a game of tic-tac-toe using shoes, socks, and bare feet on the squares of the linoleum floor.

Alice spent most of the time swiveling her head from side to side, trying to catch sight of good-looking boys, and when she'd see someone interesting, she'd turn to me and whisper a few comments. Once, midwhisper, we became aware that everyone around us had suddenly gotten quiet.

"Little girl," Captain Bob said, pointing in Alice's direction. She looked around to see who he was talking to. When she turned back, he'd taken a couple of steps toward us and was looking right at her.

"I'm not little," she said indignantly.

"Come on up front, please."

"What for?" she asked.

"Haven't we been listening?" he said in this little baby voice. "To help Captain Bob lead the Junior Fire Chief pledge."

A few minutes later, Alice was in front of the whole sixth grade, calling out lines like "Hail, Junior Fire Chief, always on guard!'' over and over again until everyone had memorized them. With each repetition, her face flushed a little more, until by the time she was done, her color exactly matched the plastic fireman's helmet Captain Bob had put on her head.

"I'm moving to another town," Alice said, staring at the ground as we walked home after school. "I'll get a new name and go to a surgeon to get my face changed. No one will know I was the person who led the Junior Fire Chief pledge."

"It wasn't that bad."

"Oh, yeah? After the assembly, Billy Wilson called me Sparky."

As usual in cases of severe depression, I recommended a trip to Speedy Burgers, my favorite fast-food joint. Alice and I had just finished splitting a large order of fries when I became aware of a shadow on the table. I looked up and found myself gazing at Kevin Reynolds. He wore a neatly pressed pair of jeans, penny loafers, and a letterman's jacket, and he was carrying a tray full of food.

"Do I know you?" he asked me.

Yes, I thought, you witnessed the most humiliating moment of my life.

"No," I said.

"You look familiar."

I shook my head. "Couldn't be. I don't know anyone at Brentwood Prep."

"What makes you think I go there?"

"Huh?" I said. "Well, uh . . ."

"The jacket," said Alice, nervously glancing back and forth between us. "*B* for Brentwood, right?"

Suddenly a smile lit up his face. "I know. You were the girl at the mall."

"Mall? What mall?"

"One of the great spills of all time," he said. "Really impressive."

"Oh, you mean the chair. And the Coke."

"And that pinwheel thing you did with your arms," he said. "The guys talked about it for days."

I wanted to curl up into a ball and roll out the door.

"Mind if I sit down?" he asked.

"Sit next to Becky!" exclaimed Alice. She winced as I kicked her under the table.

He set down his tray, then slid in next to me and introduced himself. "You know, Becky, you shouldn't worry about that spill. I've had a lot worse myself."

"Oh, sure," said Alice.

He took a bite of his hamburger. "One time, for instance, I was tossing around a football with some buddies after school. I wanted to impress a girl who was watching, so I decided to demonstrate a dropkick. That's where you drop the ball and kick it as it bounces. Well, the ball took a bad hop, and the only thing I kicked was air. My momentum took me two feet off the ground, then whap! I fell flat on my back."

"How awful," I said.

"My friends loved it. For weeks after that, they called me Dropkick."

"What about the girl?" asked Alice.

53

"I ended up going out with her for a year. She gave me a cushion as an anniversary present."

He took another big bite out of the hamburger. "So, do you go to Marshall?" Marshall was the local junior high school.

"Alice and I will be there next fall," I said.

He looked from me to Alice and back again. "You're in the same grade?"

I nodded. Alice blushed.

"How old are you?" he asked me.

"Twelve. In a few weeks."

"You go to elementary school," Kevin said, staring at me.

"She's very mature for her age," said Alice.

"I guess so," he said.

"I mean emotionally, too. She's the nicest person I know."

Kevin smiled. "What are you, her agent?"

"I'm her best friend. Isn't that right, Becky?"

I sighed. "Yes, Alice."

Kevin finished off the hamburger, then downed his soda in a few gulps. He wiped his mouth with a napkin and eyed me, as if he were trying to make up his mind.

"Would you like to go out sometime?" he asked.

"Me?"

"Don't look so surprised. Guys must ask you out all the time."

"She's very popular," said Alice.

Kicking her again, I tried to decide what I should do. What I needed was more time.

"I want to check with my parents," I said. "They're pretty strict."

"It doesn't have to be a big deal. We could just meet after school."

"I still need to ask." I wrote my phone number on a sheet of notebook paper and handed it to him. "Call me tomorrow, okay?"

He shrugged. "Sure. Hey, good to meet you. Both of you."

When he was gone, Alice turned to me, her eyes open wide. "Are you crazy?"

"I don't know. Am I?"

"Kevin Reynolds is a hunk. Half the girls in this town would trade a year's allowance for a date with that guy."

"I just wanted some time to think," I said.

"What's to think about? The correct answer is yes."

"But he's in high school."

"He's rich and handsome," she said. "And there's an unexpected bonus. He's nice."

"What about Sammy? He might feel bad."

She hit her palm against the side of her head. "I need to get my hearing checked. I thought you said you were worried about Sammy Carducci."

"Stop it. I'm serious."

Alice took my hand in both of hers. "Becky, I feel it's my duty as a friend to tell you this. You're about to make a mistake you'll regret for the rest of your life. In your situation you can do one thing and one thing only."

"And what's that?" I said.

"Go for the gold."

55

After dinner that night, I went into my room and closed the door. I thought about the letterman's jacket and the blond hair and the smiling face and the advice from my friend.

When Kevin Reynolds called the next day, I told him no.

"Really?" he said, sounding genuinely surprised.

"I'm sorry, Kevin."

"Okay, have it your way. But you need to know something about me. I don't give up easily."

# 7

# THE IFT

## ✎ Sammy

THAT BECKY, she's something. The week after the dance, she invites me over for Sunday dinner at her house. It's going to be just Becky and her parents and me, since she's got no brothers and sisters. It'll give me a chance to show off the old Carducci charm in, shall we say, a more intimate setting.

Then I catch a break. I find out Becky's birthday is coming up in a few weeks. If I bring a present to dinner, maybe I can score some points. I pick up the phone and switch my fingers to automatic, which means they dial Gus. He agrees to meet me Saturday morning on Second Avenue.

I'm standing in front of Jerry's Pawnshop when Gus rides up on his bike. He locks it next to mine by a lamppost, then glances around with a worried look on his face.

"Why can't we go to the mall like everybody else?" he asks.

"It's got no personality, that's why. Second Avenue has real stores with real people."

"Like that man lying in the gutter over there?" says Gus.

57

"The guy's harmless. He's catching a few winks, that's all."

"I hate this place," says Gus.

"Fine," I tell him. "Why don't you just get on your bike and go down to the mall with the rest of the zombies?"

He kind of shuffles his feet. "I was just kidding, Sammy," he says, giving me a weak smile.

I slap him on the back. "That's the Gus Gaffney I know."

First things first. We go to the newsstand and buy a paper, which I fold over and tuck under my arm the way I've seen Nick do. I'm not sure what it's for, but I like the way it looks. While we're there, I pick up a pack of Juicy Fruit and a box of breath mints. I pop a mint into my mouth and offer one to Gus.

"A word to the wise," I tell him.

"Huh?"

"That's like a tip. It means you could use one of these."

"Do I have bad breath?" he asks.

"Not exactly. Your breath just smells like a mouth. You want it to have a flavor. These mints happen to be menthol."

He takes a mint out of the box and holds it between two fingers. "This thing is blue," he says.

"That's the color of the menthol plant."

He puts it in his mouth and then waits, like it's going to explode or something. When it doesn't, he grins. "It tingles."

"Welcome to the modern world," I tell him.

We go past a little market and a used furniture store, sucking on our menthol breath mints. As we walk, I can feel the cool breeze whip around inside my mouth. Finally we go into a drugstore. There's a lady behind the counter watching a little TV set. She grunts as we enter the place.

I pick up a plastic shopping basket and head for one of the aisles. "The drugstore is one of the most important stores for anybody who's interested in women," I explain. "That's because of personal hygiene."

"What's that?"

I shake my head. "Just what I was afraid of. Okay, take Nick, for example. Before he goes out on a date, he spends time in the bathroom getting ready. Most of the things he uses can be found right here in the personal hygiene section of the drugstore. I'm going to buy some of this stuff so I can make a good impression on Becky tomorrow."

I take a toothbrush off the rack and show it to Gus. "Special shape. Helps you brush those hard-to-reach places." Gus looks it over and I drop it into my basket.

"Here's a pocket comb," I tell him. "You use it at home, plus you take it with you on the date. Whenever you want to look sharp, you pull it out and run it through your hair a few times."

"Wow," says Gus.

"Nose-hair scissors—very important. There's nothing women hate more than some guy who has long hairs sticking out of his nose."

"My grandfather has those. There's some in his ears, too."

"Look how the nose-hair scissors are kind of round on the end," I point out. "They're exactly in the shape of a nostril."

I pick up an emery board, nail clippers, and a pair of Odor-Eaters, and I pop them into the basket. "Nothing turns off a woman more than long fingernails that are dirty. Unless it's smelly feet.''

The next shelf is loaded with mouthwash. "This is the stuff you use when breath mints won't do the trick. A common mistake is to get the kind that tastes best.''

"What's wrong with that?''

"Use your head, Gus. If you like it, the germs will, too. Some of these brands actually attract bacteria. What you want is the worst-tasting mouthwash you can find, like this yellow stuff. It's horrible.'' I grab a big bottle and toss it in with the other personal hygiene products. "I've got another one at home, but it's always good to have a backup.

"Okay,'' I say, "now that you're clean, the next thing to do is show that you're sensitive.''

"I have a sensitive stomach,'' he says.

"I'm talking about your whole body, plus your brain. The way you do it is to buy a present.''

"Great!'' says Gus, all excited. He runs over to the toy section and picks out a remote-control tank. "Becky would love this.''

"Gus, let me explain something. Women aren't interested in a tank. To start with, it's not pink.''

"Here's a pink Corvette.''

"Pretend you're this woman who likes mushy TV shows and stuff like that,'' I tell him. "What do you want somebody to buy you?''

He looks wildly around. "A baseball?''

"Think about it, Gus.''

"A softball?''

"Let me give you a few examples of things women like,'' I say, walking down the aisle. "Bic pens. Umbrellas. Any kind of candy bar with marshmallows in it. Socks with little dangly things. Notebook paper. Fabric softener. Use your imagination, Gus.''

He thinks about it for a minute, then goes over to a rack and picks out a pair of black plastic sunglasses. The tag hangs down over his nose.

"What do you think?'' he says.

"Keep looking,'' I tell him.

He stares in the mirror at the top of the rack, smoothing his hair. "But these are so cool.''

I turn the corner and stop in my tracks. I'm face-to-face with the perfect gift. There's a whole bunch of them stacked on this big display. It's exactly what I've been looking for.

A quart of perfume.

It's called Secret Desire. At the top of the label it says *Giant Economy Size*. It's even pink.

"This is great,'' I say, taking one of the bottles. "It'll last her a year. Every time she pours some on, she'll think of me.''

We go to the counter. The lady doesn't even look up from her little TV set. She's on the chubby side, and she's wearing something that could either be a dress or a bathrobe. There's a smell kind of like wine coming from somewhere in the area.

"Pardon me,'' I say.

As she turns toward us, one eye trails along behind the other one. When we have her attention, Gus buys the sunglasses, which he's decided to keep for himself. I pay for my things and tell her to gift wrap the perfume. She disappears into a back room.

I'm feeling pretty good, so I challenge Gus to an arm-

61

wrestling match while we're waiting. I win six in a row, but it's not much fun because I'm afraid of crushing the bones in his scrawny arm.

Finally the lady comes out of the back room with my stuff. The mouthwash is in one bag, the personal hygiene articles are in another, and the perfume is gift wrapped in white paper with little storks on it. I have to admit it looks sharp.

"Can I have some of that mouthwash?" Gus asks me when we get outside.

"On a city street? Grow up."

"Come on, Sammy, just a sip." He glances down at the sidewalk, like he's embarrassed. "I've never tried any before."

"Oh, for crying out loud." I look around to see if the coast is clear. "Okay, but make it fast. And don't show the bottle."

While I unlock my bike, Gus reaches into the mouth-wash bag, unscrews the cap without looking, and raises the bottle until the top is just barely poking out. He takes some into his mouth and swishes it around. Suddenly he turns his head away and sprays the stuff all over the sidewalk.

"This tastes terrible!" he says.

"Of course it does. That's why I bought it." I put away my bicycle lock and flip up the kickstand. As Gus puts the cap back on and hands me the bag, he keeps spitting and shuddering.

"Better get used to it," I tell him. "You're going to be using a lot of that stuff."

— ◆ —

My mom takes me to Becky's house Sunday afternoon. She wants to go to the door with me and say hello, which makes my blood run cold.

"You think Sinatra's mother goes to the door with him?" I ask. That seems to do the trick. She agrees to drop me off around the corner.

I pull a toothpick out of my pocket and stick it in my mouth, then walk up to the front door, taking my time the way Nick might do. I'm carrying the gift-wrapped perfume in a bag, which I swing at my side. When I ring the doorbell, Mrs. Davidson answers. She flashes me a big smile.

"Come on in," she says.

"Don't mind if I do."

She looks up and down the street. "How did you get here?"

"Cab."

"Hi, Sammy." It's Becky, looking stupendous as usual. She's wearing a plain yellow dress, but on her it doesn't look plain. "What's in the bag?"

"Oh, nothing."

"Can I take it for you?"

"That's okay; I'll just carry it."

We go in the living room, where Mr. Davidson looks up from his Sunday paper.

"Great article on lawn maintenance," he tells me as I sit down across from him.

"Yeah, I saw that," I tell him.

Mrs. Davidson disappears into the kitchen. Becky, Mr. Davidson, and I shoot the breeze for a few minutes. As we talk, I can't help but notice how neat the place is. If our house was this neat, it would mean we all died.

I hear a bell. "Is that your door? You expecting some-body?"

Becky laughs. "That's not the doorbell. It means five minutes till dinner. Do you want to wash your hands?"

"Huh? Oh, yeah. I'm big on personal hygiene."

I wash my hands, wondering what kind of people ring a warning bell before dinner. There's something creepy about it, like a movie I saw once where aliens rent a house and pose as a normal family. I go into the dining room, trying to push the thought out of my head.

When I get there, the food is on the table, and Becky and her folks are standing behind their chairs. We all sit down, with Becky across from me and her parents on either side. I put the toothpick back in my pocket and set my bag down by the chair.

It turns out to be the strangest dinner on record. Becky's mom and dad ask me all sorts of questions about myself, which is fine, but when I ask them something, the subject always comes back to their house. I learn more about wall-paper than I ever wanted to know. The food's unusual, too. There's kind of a dried-out hamburger patty that Mrs. Davidson calls a Salisbury steak, and Mr. Davidson can't stop raving about how great it is. There are mashed potatoes, and everybody has a little green salad, which I hardly rec-ognize because it doesn't have any olives. The zucchini is okay, but there's no tomato sauce to put on it. For dessert we each get a dish of ice cream, and when Becky points out that it's vanilla, everybody chuckles. I have no idea what's so funny, but figuring they're in a good mood, I reach down by my chair and open up the bag.

64

"This is for you," I say, handing Becky my package. "It's kind of like a birthday present."

"Sammy, this is so sweet. How did you know?"

"I got my sources."

"Are those storks on the wrapping paper?" Mrs. Davidson asks.

"Yeah, I think so. Nice, huh?"

For some reason, she turns away from the table for a second. Becky smiles a little. "Yes, Sammy, it's very nice."

Becky starts unwrapping the gift. "Can you give me a hint about what it is?"

I shrug. "Let's just say it has something to do with smell."

She tears away a little piece of paper, then a little more so she can read the label. Suddenly she gets this funny look on her face. She's obviously overwhelmed by my generosity.

I shrug modestly. "It's a big bottle. I figured you'd want a lot."

She tears off the rest of the paper and turns it around so her parents can see what's inside.

It's the mouthwash.

"There's been a mistake!" I screech. "It was supposed to be perfume. Swear to God!"

Suddenly I know what must have happened. The dipsy lady at the drugstore mixed up the two bottles and wrapped the mouthwash by accident.

At least it explains one thing. Gus was right when he said the mouthwash tasted terrible. He had been gargling with Secret Desire.

65

I get ready to make a break for the door and escape to my house, where I'll go in the closet and not come out for two hundred years. Then I notice something. Mr. and Mrs. Davidson are laughing. In fact, they're practically falling on the floor.

Mr. Davidson hoots, "Well, you said you were big on personal hygiene."

"And it does have something to do with smell," gasps Mrs. Davidson.

Becky looks at me and giggles, then takes off the bottle cap and dabs some mouthwash behind her ears. That gets me going, and before you know it, the four of us are laughing our heads off. It almost hurts, I'm laughing so hard. The crazy thing is, it goes on for three, maybe four minutes. It's like there was all this pressure built up from everybody trying to act so nice, and now we can let it out.

When it's over, we just kind of sit around with silly grins on our faces, trying to get our breath. Every once in a while we catch each other's eye and start laughing again. Finally we all get up and clear off the dishes.

We spend the rest of the afternoon sitting around the living room, talking. It turns out Becky and her folks laugh a lot. Part of the time I'm the one they're laughing at, but it doesn't bother me because the rest of the group gets their turn, too. Becky calls her folks Mr. and Mrs. Suburbia, and everybody gets a big kick out of that. Her parents take me around the house and show me all their projects, which turn out to be pretty exciting.

Well, not really.

# THE GANG

### ✎ Becky

"GRANDMA," said Sammy, "this is Becky Davidson."

I smiled at the old woman, and she smiled back. I could tell she'd had a handsome face when she was younger.

"How come you so big and Sammy so little?" she asked me.

"Do you mind?" said Sammy. He turned to me. "She always says whatever she's thinking."

"That's okay," I said.

"Hey," said Sammy, pulling me away, "there's Nick. Excuse us, Grandma."

Sammy had invited me to his house for a Carducci family dinner. I'd imagined ten or twelve people sitting around the table, with maybe a few kids playing in the yard. Instead, it was Grand Central Station at rush hour. The hallways were jammed with people talking loud and waving their hands. Thousands of children careened through the house at full speed. In the kitchen, teams of women shuttled food from the refrigerator to the oven, stopping every so often to sip from tumblers of red wine. A group was playing badminton in the backyard, and when the birdie hit the

67

ground, a little boy would grab it and run. Another group was playing video games in the den, and someone kept yelling, "You die! You die!"

"Are you okay?" Sammy asked me. "You look kinda green around the gills."

"Are your family dinners always like this?"

He looked around. "No, it's quiet today."

We found Sammy's brother, Nick, lounging on a sofa in front of the TV, his arm draped casually around an attractive blonde. They were watching the shopper's channel.

"Yo, Nick," said Sammy.

Nick kept staring at the screen. "You should watch this, kiddo. Some very good deals. A minute ago they had a VCR for only ninety-nine bucks. I've seen it advertised for two-fifty."

Sammy looked at the blonde and grinned. "Cindy, remember me? I'm Nick's brother, Sammy."

"Sure," Cindy said, smiling vaguely.

"And this is my friend Becky," said Sammy. Cindy nodded in my direction.

"You think I'd look good in that tie?" Nick asked her.

"It's hard to tell with this TV," said Cindy. "Are the stripes red or pink?"

Nick shrugged. "Four bucks, how can you go wrong?"

There was a whirring noise from the kitchen. "What's that?" I asked.

"Electric knife," said Sammy. "My dad must be cutting up the turkey. Come on, I'll introduce you."

We squeezed through the mob in front of the oven and made our way to the kitchen table, where a short, slight, curly-haired woman was preparing a relish tray. Next to her, a thin man with a strong jaw was carving a turkey.

"Here, Pop," said Sammy, "let me give you a hand with that."

"I got it, Sammy."

"No, really, I could do that whole turkey in two minutes flat." When Sammy didn't get a response, he tugged at his father's arm.

"Sammy, you're getting on my nerves."

"You don't even trust your own son?"

Mr. Carducci switched off the knife and put one hand on his hip. He looked down at Sammy, then noticed me.

"Oh," said Sammy, "this is Becky Davidson."

Mr. Carducci gazed at me for a moment, then smiled. It was as if the clouds had lifted and the sun had burst through.

"I'd shake hands," he said, indicating the knife, "but I might be dangerous."

"I'll do the honors for both of us," said the curly-haired woman, wiping off her hands and shaking mine. "I'm Lynn Carducci. I heard you two had a nice time at the dance."

"Yeah, things are never dull with Sammy around."

"That's one way of putting it," said Mr. Carducci.

Sammy slapped his father on the back. "Admit it, Pop, you worship the ground I walk on."

"How can such a little kid be too big for his britches?" said Mr. Carducci, turning back to the turkey. He started up the knife again, and Sammy started up his mouth.

"You might want to cut those slices thinner," he told his father.

"Becky," said Mrs. Carducci, "would you like to see my flower garden?"

I nodded and followed her out the back door and around the side of the house to a place where there were no people, dogs, or TV sets. There were only rosebushes, three neat rows of them, with pink and yellow blossoms. I could feel myself relax for the first time since I'd arrived.

"You're feeling a little overwhelmed, aren't you?" said Mrs. Carducci.

"Was it that obvious?"

"No, I'm just familiar with the signs. I used to see them in the mirror every day."

"I like your flower garden," I said.

"It's my retreat. I come out here and work whenever I need some quiet time, which around here is pretty often."

I leaned down and sniffed one of the blossoms. "It reminds me of my Aunt Ella. She always keeps roses on her table."

"They're wonderful people, you know. The Carduccis, I mean."

"You're a Carducci, aren't you?" I said.

"Now I am. But it took a while. I was raised in a home where we said 'please' and 'thank you' and not much else."

"Really?"

She nodded. "The Carduccis can be loud and sometimes even obnoxious, but they have good hearts. I wanted to make certain you knew that."

When we went back inside, Sammy was at it again. Dinner was being laid out cafeteria style on two long tables with red plastic tablecloths, and he'd taken it on himself to direct traffic.

"Does that look like the pasta section?" he called out to

70

a chubby, dark-haired woman. "Pasta down here, for crying out loud."

"Sammy, calm down, huh?" said his father as he walked past.

"Don't worry, Pop, I got it under control."

When the food was on the table, Sammy and I took plates and got in line. I looked over the two tables. "I've never seen so much food in my life."

"Around here we do things big," he said. "We got spaghetti, eggplant parmigiana, manicotti, provolone, fried cauliflower, stromboli, stuffed artichokes—you'll like those."

By the time I reached the end of the second table, my plate was piled four inches high with food.

"This is embarrassing," I said.

"Don't worry; you can come back for more."

We poured ourselves some soda, and then Sammy led the way into the living room, where rows of tables had been set up. He spotted a couple of seats next to Nick, and we moved off in that direction.

"Kids in the den, Sammy," his father called from across the room.

Laughing, Sammy said, "I'm too old for that, Pop."

"You know the rule. Sixteen and under."

"I got a date. That makes me exempt." Sammy set his plate down on the table.

Sighing, Mr. Carducci walked over and pulled Sammy aside. I couldn't hear what he said, but when he finished, Sammy picked up his plate and went into the den.

Sitting down next to Sammy, I noticed that his shoulders

71

were hunched over and his eyes downcast. In a gentle voice, I asked, "What are you thinking, Sammy?"

"Hm? Oh, I was just trying to figure how to sneak some wine out of the kitchen."

Kevin Reynolds called me the next day. When he asked me out again, I told him no. I told him no the day after that, and the day after that, too. I guess it was an answer he wasn't used to hearing.

The following weekend I was at the mall by myself, looking through some magazines at the bookstore, when I heard a familiar voice.

"Alone at last."

I turned around and saw Kevin. "Are you following me?"

"No, but it's not a bad idea. How are you doing?"

"You should know. We've talked every day this week."

"I don't give up easily," he said, grinning. "Which reminds me, want to go to the Rialto Friday night? They're showing one of my favorite movies."

"Look, Kevin, this is really flattering, but I can't go out with you. Please don't keep asking me."

"Okay, I'll stop asking—on one condition. Come to the food park with me and have a soda."

"Right now?"

"You'll be perfectly safe. If you fall, I'll catch you."

"Very funny," I said.

"Is it a deal?"

"No more calls? Promise?"

"I swear on a stack of phone books," he said.

"All right, then. But only for a few minutes."

# THE FREEZE

## ✏ Sammy

GET A LOAD of this. The day after the big family dinner, Gus informs me he wants to go shopping, which is nothing unusual. Then he tells me what it's for.

A present for Alice Biddle.

"I'm getting ready to make my move," he says.

I can hardly believe this is my friend Gus Gaffney talking. He sounds like a whole new man.

"That's great!" I tell him. "You gonna get perfume?"

He shakes his head. "Perfume's okay if they don't hate you. I need something better than that. Something really incredible."

"Like what?"

"I'm not sure," he says, "but I'll know it when I see it."

Then he tells me where he wants to shop. I can't believe my ears. "The mall? That place is the pits. Let's go down to Second Avenue."

"There aren't enough stores. Come on, Sammy, please?"

He gives me such a pathetic look that I finally give in, against my better judgment.

"Okay," I tell him, "but if we turn into zombies, it's your fault."

When we get to the mall, we start on the bottom level and go down the row of stores, stopping in every one of them to see if anything hits Gus just right. He even goes in the paint store.

"What could you get here?" I ask.

"I don't know. Brushes, putty, a gallon of paint. You can never tell when something's going to jump out at you."

"It better not jump out on my suit," I tell him.

Halfway down the third row of stores, I'm starting to wonder if he'll ever find anything.

"Plenty of perfume," I point out as we cruise through a drugstore. "Too bad the bottles are so little."

When we duck into the next store, Gus starts jumping up and down and clapping his hands.

"This is it!" he says in a little squealy voice.

"Geez, Gus, try to control yourself." I look around to make sure nobody I know is watching.

"It's perfect!"

I don't know how perfect it is, but I'm glad to see Gus following one of my tips: Dare to be different.

"Okay," I ask him when we get to his house, "what are you going to say when you give this present to her?"

"What do you mean?"

"You can't just walk up and dump it in her lap. You gotta have a conversation."

He gets this pinched look on his face. "My stomach hurts."

I put my arm around his shoulders. "Gus, there's a very simple answer to your problem."

74

"I know," he says. "Tums."

"No, practice. That's the secret of talking to women."

"Who am I going to practice on?"

I give it some thought, then snap my fingers. "Of course. She'll be perfect."

Which is how we end up offering Gus's seven-year-old sister a dollar to pretend she's Alice Biddle.

"Hurry up, okay?" says Gretchen. "My favorite TV show comes on pretty soon."

"Okay," Gus asks me, "what do I do?"

"The important thing to remember is, you want to make a good first impression."

"I can put on some of my dad's after-shave," he says, starting down the hallway.

"I'm telling," Gretchen calls out after him.

"That's all right, Gus," I say. "It's probably better to use the magnetic force of your personality."

"I tried that at the dance. I even gave her the Eye. You saw what happened."

"Okay, so we need a new approach. Tell her some amazing facts. That always starts things off on a good note."

"I don't know any amazing facts," he says.

"Here's one." I whisper it in his ear.

Gus turns to his sister. "Did you know there was a man in Butte, Montana, who built a car out of sardine cans?"

"I hate sardines."

I whisper another amazing fact to Gus.

"Toy poodles are alien monsters from outer space," he tells his sister.

"Are we done yet?" she asks.

I'm worried we're losing her, so I say to Gus, "Time to bring out the big guns. Mainly, the voice of love."

"Is this the one that drives women nuts?"

"Guaranteed. Okay, when you hear me talk again, it'll be the voice of love."

I close my eyes and massage the sides of my neck with my fingers; then I push my chin down into my chest. I try to picture Nick with his arm around Cindy, talking about his Grand Am.

"Alice," I say, "you're very beautiful."

"How'd you do that?" asks Gus. "You sound like Artie Mayfield at summer camp. He had an operation on his throat."

"Look, you want me to help you or not?" I say. "This thing works, trust me."

"Sure, Sammy, sure." Gus rubs his neck and lowers his chin. "Alice, you're very beautiful."

"Can I go now?" Gretchen asks.

I slap Gus on the back. "That was perfect. From now on, you're a dangerous man."

Gus beams. I peel off a dollar bill and hand it to Gretchen. "Go buy yourself something nice, sweetheart."


Friday after school we ride our bikes over to Alice's street. I hide behind a tree, and Gus waits for Alice to come home from her job at the library. Sure enough, about four o'clock she turns the corner. Gus meets up with her right in front of my tree. So far, so good. Everything's going like clockwork.

"Uh, Alice—" Gus says in this trembly voice. He's holding the gift behind his back so she can't see it.

76

"You little sneak," says Alice. "Have you been hanging around my house?"

I can tell it throws Gus off. "Toy poodles are aliens from outer space," he says, falling back on amazing facts.

"You better get off this block," says Alice. "And for your information, my mother and I own a poodle."

Gus quickly massages his neck and puts his chin down on his chest, but Alice pushes past him.

"Hey, wait!" Gus says in the voice of love. It comes out sounding more like a seal barking. When she doesn't stop, he pulls out the gift. It's a shoebox with a ribbon tied around it and holes punched in the side. "I brought something for you."

Alice turns around and says, "What's that?" She's suddenly looking friendlier, which gives Gus a boost.

"Oh, just a little present."

As she takes it, Gus grins. He glances over at me, and I give him the thumbs-up. Alice stops for a second before opening the present, like she's wondering what she's getting herself into. Then she shrugs and tears off the ribbon.

"I wanted to get you something special," says Gus. "When I saw this, I knew it was perfect."

She takes off the top and peeks inside. Her jaw drops open as she looks at the gift we searched and searched for at the mall, the one that jumped out at us when we walked into the store.

It's a lizard.

"I named it Alice," says Gus proudly.

Meanwhile, the real Alice just stares. I get the feeling she doesn't hear a word of what Gus is saying.

"The man at the pet store said it's easy to take care of," Gus babbles happily. "It's got its own little leash and—"

Alice screams. Snapping out of her trance, she drops the box on the ground and runs around the area in little circles, shaking her hands.

The lizard jumps from the box and takes off down the sidewalk. Gus scrambles after it, calling, "Alice, here, Alice."

I poke my head out from behind the tree to get a better view of the action. Unfortunately, Alice picks that moment to glance over in my direction.

"You little pervert!" she says. "You think this is funny, don't you?"

It hits me that I'm grinning like a madman. I try to wipe the smile off my face, but it keeps springing back.

Alice walks toward me with her finger pointed like a loaded gun. "I bet you planned this whole thing. You couldn't wait to see what I'd do when I opened the package."

"Alice, you got me all wrong."

"You think you're a big shot," she says, "but the closest you ever got was when you went out with Becky. And that's never going to happen again because now she's dating a real big shot. His name is Kevin Reynolds, and he goes to Brentwood Prep."

I guess I stop grinning, because she smiles. Then she puts her nose in the air and walks off.

Just about that time Gus comes racing back, holding the lizard high in triumph. "I've decided to keep it," he says. "Only I'm renaming it Godzilla."

I can't share his moment of happiness because I'm thinking about this so-called big shot Kevin Reynolds. I wonder if Becky really is dating him.

Finally I decide that's ridiculous. Alice is just trying to make me mad. If Becky's going out with somebody else, she would tell me.

It turns out Gus's mom doesn't want anything named Godzilla running around her house, and she tells Gus to return it. On Saturday we go to the pet shop, where I'm a little surprised the owner agrees to take back a used lizard. Then Gus drags me around the mall again, looking for more stuff to buy. After an hour or so, I can't stand it anymore. My feet are tired, and my throat's dry from breathing zombie air.

"Is there anyplace we can get something to drink in this dump?" I ask him.

"Sure. Come on."

We head over toward a bunch of tables surrounded by little food stands. We're standing in line when Gus points to a table across the way.

"Hey, isn't that Becky?"

At first her back is to us, so I can't tell for sure. Then she turns so we can see the side of her face.

It's Becky, all right. And she's sitting across from a guy wearing a Brentwood Prep letterman's jacket.

As I stare in shock, the guy smiles at her and she smiles back. I want to punch out his beautiful teeth, but I manage to control myself. Lucky for him.

"It's her," says Gus. "Hey, B—"

I clamp my hand over his mouth. "Let's watch them for a minute."

They talk a little bit longer, then get up from the table

and walk over to the elevator. They get in, and the doors close behind them.

"Quick!" I say to Gus. We dodge through the tables, and when we reach the elevator, I pound the button with my fist. A green arrow lights up. Half a minute later, we're still staring at the arrow. I look around and spot the escalator. We hurry over and race down the moving stairs, bumping people as we go.

"Medical emergency," I tell the people. I'm not sure they buy it.

On the next level down, we go to the elevator but don't see Becky or the guy. We split up and search the mall for the next ten minutes, checking both levels and the parking garage. There's no sign of them.

"Let's get out of here," I tell Gus. "I hate this stupid place."

At home that night I try to watch TV, but all I can see is a picture of Becky and El Creepo sitting at that table, grinning at each other like a couple of saps.

Nick comes in and wants to watch a detective show. I tell him sure. I figure it doesn't matter, since I'll see the same picture on every channel.

"How's it going with Cindy?" I ask him.

"What do you care?" he says, staring at the tube.

"Nick, you're my man. What happens to you happens to me."

He watches an undercover cop kick in a door and spray a warehouse with bullets. "She kept dropping hints about marriage and kids. It was getting on my nerves. I told her to give it a rest."

"Wow, really straightened her out, huh?"

The cop collars a drug dealer and drags him out of the warehouse. "You gotta stay in control of the situation, Sammy," says Nick. "Always."

When I see Gus the next day, he asks me how I'm doing.

"Great," I tell him.

"I thought you felt bad about Becky."

"Gus, let me explain something. When you're dealing with women, you gotta be in control of the situation. If something's bothering you, you don't sit around crying about it. You just do what needs to be done. Period."

"So what are you going to do?" he asks.

"She's left me no choice. It's time to use the Freeze."

"What's that?"

"The most deadly weapon a man can use on a woman. She's going to regret ever setting eyes on that jerk."

Gus stares at me in awe.

"Of course," I go on, "that's just phase one. Phase two is observation. That means checking up on her to see the devastating effect of the Freeze."

"How do we do that?"

"Follow her."

"This is so cool," says Gus.

"Stick around," I tell him. "It could get interesting."

# 10

# THE SQUEEZE

✎ Becky

I SAW SAMMY in the school cafeteria Monday and waved. "How was your weekend?" I called.

A funny thing happened. He looked through me, as if I were invisible. Then he took a pair of dark glasses from his pocket, put them on, and walked right past me.

I was too surprised to move. I just stood there, with kids brushing by on either side, and watched him leave.

The rest of the day didn't go too well. I missed six out of ten problems on an arithmetic quiz. I accidentally called Mr. Lawrence "Dad." During a discussion I said that Christopher Columbus was the first president of the United States.

When the three o'clock bell rang, I hurried toward Mrs. McNulty's room. As I approached, I saw Sammy coming out the door and planted myself in his path.

"I need to talk to you," I said. He slipped on his dark glasses again and, without looking at me, veered off to the side.

"Sammy, what's the matter?" I asked as he went by. He didn't say a thing.

I caught up to him and followed alongside. "Are you mad at me?" No answer. "You could at least look at me, you know." When he didn't, I moved in front of him again and started walking backward, leaning down and peering into his face.

"Hello in there. Yoo-hoo. Anybody home?" All I saw was my reflection in his glasses. I started making faces, hoping to get a reaction. I stretched my mouth and squinted my eyes and wiggled my fingers in my ears. He just stared blankly ahead, as if I were a ghost.

I bumped into someone, almost losing my balance, and turned around to see Mr. Lawrence.

"Becky, what's your problem today?" he asked.

"Nothing, Mr. Lawrence," I said, feeling myself turn bright red.

"We're funny in this school. We like to walk facing the front."

"Yes, sir, I'm sorry." I turned around and, spotting Sammy straight ahead, caught up to him.

"Great," I said. "Thanks to you, my teacher thinks I'm turning into a flake."

Sammy just kept walking.

"I can wait you out, Sammy Carducci. I'm going to stay right beside you until you say something. I'll be like your shadow. I'll go wherever you go."

He hung a left and went into the one place where I couldn't follow.

"That's right," I shouted at him from outside. "The boys' bathroom, refuge of the weak."

I became aware of people watching me. One of them

83

was Gus Gaffney. When I moved toward him, he put on his own pair of dark glasses and started to hurry off.

"Oh, no, you don't," I said, catching up in three long strides. I reached over and snatched off the glasses. Watching him cringe, I had an idea.

"Could I buy you some ice cream?" I said.

"Huh? Really?"

"Order anything you want. I thought maybe you and I could get to know each other."

He glanced back over his shoulder. "I guess that would be okay. Could I get a chocolate sundae?"

A couple of minutes later, I had him eating out of my hand. Actually, it was an ice cream dish.

"So, Gus," I said, "you seem to be pretty good friends with Sammy."

He nodded. "Sammy and me, we're like that." He tried putting two fingers together to demonstrate what he meant but couldn't figure out which ones to use.

"He sure is a nice guy," I said.

"The thing I can't believe," said Gus, "is how he always knows what to do in every situation."

"He sure does. Like today, for instance. No matter what I said to him, he wouldn't talk to me at all."

Gus grinned. "It's called the Freeze. It's the most deadly weapon a man can use on a woman."

"Oh, really? Why is he using it on me?"

Gus got a crafty look on his face, then checked the area to make sure no one was listening. "He knows about you and that high school guy. The one at the mall."

Sammy had seen me with Kevin Reynolds. I felt a surge of regret that I'd ever sat down with Kevin.

"See," said Gus, "when you're dealing with women, you always have to be in control of the situation. That's what Sammy says."

"He does?"

Gus nodded. "That's because women are weak. They need somebody strong."

"This is interesting. What else does he say?"

"Oh, different things. Women cry a lot, of course. They go around in groups so they'll have somebody to talk to. They're mushy."

My regrets about Kevin were fading. "Sammy told you all this?"

"Sure," said Gus. "He gave me a whole page of tips about impressing women. He covered everything—after-shave, umbrellas, you name it."

"Umbrellas?"

"He even taught me the voice of love. Women go crazy over it."

As he spoke, Gus was using his spoon to carve the ice cream into a shape of some kind. I couldn't tell what it was supposed to be, but it was square and had raised areas at the corners.

"How long do you think this Freeze will go on?" I asked.

"Don't know. I guess it depends on what he finds out from phase two."

"Which is?"

"Observation."

"You mean he's going to follow me?" I asked, trying to hide my rising anger.

Gus suddenly looked nervous. "No, I don't think so.

Nope. Definitely not." He gulped down the ice cream, funny shape and all, then got to his feet. "I need to go."

"Did you like that chocolate sundae?" I asked him.

"Oh, yeah. Thanks."

"You know where they have the best sundaes? At that ice cream shop right across from the Rialto Theater. You should try it sometime."

"Maybe I will," he said, quickly gathering up his things.

"You know," I said casually, "speaking of the Rialto, I'm going to be there Friday night with that high school guy you saw at the mall."

I watched for the light in Gus's eyes. It took a few seconds, but finally a tiny bulb flickered on. He looked at me slyly. "Friday night?"

I nodded. "Well, it was good talking to you."

As I headed off, Gus darted down the street in the direction of Sammy Carducci's house. I was confident that within the hour Sammy would be planning an observation session for Friday night.

If he wanted a show, I'd give him one.

Kevin picked me up promptly at seven o'clock in a big black Mercedes. He and I rode in back behind Mrs. Reynolds, a heavy woman with a sleek fur coat and a tired smile.

"Your parents seem nice," Kevin told me.

"Yeah, they're a lot of fun, especially if you're into household appliances."

As a matter of fact, they were jumpy, and they'd been that way ever since finding out about Kevin. It had taken all my powers of persuasion to convince them I was old enough to go out with a high school boy, and my dad still wasn't sold on the idea.

"I'm glad you called back," Kevin said. "What made you change your mind?"

"A boy I know."

"Tell him thanks the next time you see him."

That may be sooner than you can imagine, I thought.

We turned off the interstate and entered the Village, a popular area full of restaurants, gift shops, and trendy clothing stores. As we pulled up in front of the Rialto Theater, I saw no sign of Sammy. Then I noticed two small figures in trench coats standing in the shadows off to one side. Wearing dark glasses and hats, they looked like a couple of miniature FBI agents. Gus had delivered my message, it seemed, and had even come along to help.

I took Kevin's arm as we got out of the car, figuring that would get a reaction from our observers. "The movie doesn't start for a while," I said. "Why don't we take a little stroll?"

He agreed, and we set off down the crowded sidewalk. I glanced backward and saw the FBI agents huddling to discuss this unexpected development. A moment later, they pulled up their collars and set out to follow us. They scurried over behind a lamppost, then darted to a mailbox. Spotting a fat woman in a bulky sweater, they slipped behind her, peeking out every so often to make sure we were still there. Meanwhile I chatted away happily, following their progress out of the corner of my eye.

"Oh, no," I said, stopping suddenly.

"What's wrong?" asked Kevin.

"I think I dropped some money."

87

I turned around and retraced my steps, pretending to scan the ground, and Kevin did the same. Just as I'd hoped, the fat woman was coming right toward us. She moved aside to go around, and all at once the FBI was exposed for all the world to see. They stood there, frozen, like a couple of rabbits caught in the glare of approaching headlights. Pretending not to see them, I chose that moment to crouch down and pick up my phantom money.

"Here it is," I said, and watched two pairs of sneakers beat a hasty exit. I took Kevin's arm again, and we resumed our walk.

"There's an ice cream shop across the street," I said as we reached the corner. "How about a cone?"

"Sure," said Kevin. "My treat."

I timed it so we entered the crosswalk just before the DON'T WALK sign flashed on. When we reached the other side, the light was turning yellow. Behind us, horns honked and two small figures scooted across the street. Inside the shop I picked out my flavor at the counter, then looked back just in time to see the FBI, which had been using the front window for observation, dive for cover.

I took Kevin's hand as we left the shop, and we followed a zigzag route back to the Rialto. As I had figured, the mysterious agents were forced to take a couple of zigs for our every zag, so by the time we reached the box office, their trench coats were starting to droop. They bought tickets and followed us into the theater, where Kevin and I took seats toward the back.

As we waited for the movie to begin, Kevin told me about Brentwood Prep and some of his school activities— lacrosse, track, debating club, student council. I didn't

88

know what half the stuff was, but it sure sounded impressive. When he asked about me, I described my family and left it at that, figuring he wouldn't be too interested in life at an elementary school.

Finally the lights dimmed, and I noticed our pursuers using the cover of darkness to slip into the seats behind us. Each of them had a jumbo soda, and I heard Gus whisper, "I wanted popcorn, too."

"Ssh!" said Sammy.

"But—" There was a pause. "Okay, okay."

Kevin reached over and put his arm around me. No boy had ever done that before, but I tried to pretend there was nothing to it. I could hear the springs in Sammy's seat creaking as he fidgeted behind me.

Well, I thought, time for the show to start.

For a minute I wasn't sure I'd be able to work up the nerve, but then I remembered some of Sammy's pronouncements and started getting mad. Before I could change my mind, I closed my eyes and did it.

I kissed Kevin Reynolds.

It was just a quick one on the cheek, but it seemed to get a good reaction because there was a sharp intake of breath from the seat behind me. Unfortunately, that wasn't the only reaction it got. The next thing I knew, Kevin was kissing me back, and this one wasn't quick. Sammy made a low gurgling sound, like you might hear from a wounded animal, and for a moment I was pleased.

But Kevin wasn't stopping. I tried to pull away, and the arm around my shoulder tightened. It occurred to me, too late, that I'd probably been encouraging him all evening, first by taking his arm, then by holding his hand, and finally by kissing him. Struggling to get free, I vowed never to touch another boy as long as I lived.

There was a splash, and Kevin's grip suddenly loosened. It was such a relief that at first I didn't think about what had happened. Then I became aware of someone standing behind Kevin's seat holding an upside-down soda cup. It was Sammy.

"Get your hands off her!" he yelled.

Kevin jumped to his feet and shook himself off, the way our cocker spaniel does when he's wet. Kevin untucked his shirttail, and ice cubes came clattering out onto the floor. Then he turned to confront Sammy.

"You little—" sputtered Kevin.

"He didn't mean it, sir," said Gus, who was crouching on his seat with his knees to his chest.

"Don't worry, Becky," said Sammy. "If this guy tries any more funny business, I'll deck him."

Kevin glanced at me, confused. "You know him?"

"Hey, shut up back there!" somebody yelled.

"Maybe you guys should sit down," said Gus.

"He's a friend from school," I said. "Both of them are."

Sammy crumpled the paper cup and waved it toward Kevin. "Yeah, and it's a lucky thing for Becky we just happened to be sitting here. You were off base, Slimeball."

Kevin leaped for him. Sprawling across the row of seats, he grabbed the lapels of Sammy's trench coat. As he jerked Sammy toward him, Sammy pulled his head back and then rammed Kevin's nose with his forehead. Kevin let go and put his hands to his nose. They came away bloody.

"Break it up!" somebody shouted.

The sight of blood seemed to do something to Kevin.

Bellowing like a bull, he vaulted into Sammy's row and started to pummel him. There were shouts and screams as people scattered.

I leaned over the back of my seat, gripped Kevin's arm, and yelled, "Stop it!" He shook me off and kept punching.

Most of the blows landed on Sammy's shoulders and chest, but one quick jab struck him squarely in the left eye. Sammy cried out, and suddenly there was Gus, jumping onto Kevin's back. The force of his landing toppled Kevin sideways, and the three of them fell into the aisle.

The movie went off, the lights went on, and the theater manager, a large man with a crew cut and tie, came running down the aisle, followed by a couple of guys from the concession stand. When the manager reached the brawlers, he pulled Gus off the pile and yanked a bloody Kevin up by the arm.

"What are you kids, crazy?" he screamed.

Sammy staggered to his feet, his left eye already starting to close. "Are you okay?" he asked me.

When I nodded, he looked over at Kevin. "Hey, Bozo, your nose is red."

Kevin lunged, but the manager grabbed and subdued him with the help of the two concessionaires.

Sammy brushed off his coat. "Get him out of my sight."

"Sir," I told the manager, "I know all these boys. There won't be any more trouble."

"Oh, there'll be a lot more trouble," said the manager. "I promise you that."

# THE END

## ✎ Sammy

ALL I CAN SAY is, that guy Kevin Reynolds should consider himself lucky they stopped the fight. I was just starting to get warmed up. I mean, I hadn't even tried my
karate yet. A couple of well-placed chops and the guy's
history.

Anyway, the theater manager and his flunkies grab the
three of us and move us up the aisle. Becky gets her purse
and comes along.

The manager calls out to the crowd, "Sorry, folks, we'll
have the movie going again in a minute."

He drags us into his office, a crummy little place that
smells like stale cigarettes, and plops down behind a metal
desk. Becky sits in a folding chair, and Kevin stands in the
corner looking nervous. Gus is next to him, twitching like
he stuck his finger in an electrical socket. Me, I casually
lean up against the wall and pull out a pack of gum.

"Juicy Fruit, anybody?"

The manager glares at me, lights up a cigarette, and leans
forward across the desk. "I'll make this quick. I'm calling
a cab for the young lady, and the rest of you will place a

phone call to your parents. You'll tell them what happened and have them come down here to pick you up.''

Picturing my dad's face, I just about swallow my gum. I notice that Gus has turned white, and Kevin is blinking real fast.

"Sir—" says Kevin.

"No discussion. If you don't like it, my next call is to the police."

A half hour later, Becky is gone and the parents start to arrive. First are Mr. and Mrs. Gaffney, who look dazed by the thought that their son was in a fight. In a funny way, Mr. Gaffney almost looks happy, especially when he sees the size of the guy Gus was up against. My dad shows up after they leave, and I can see I'm in for one of his lectures.

Before we leave, Mr. Reynolds walks in. The first thing that hits me is his clothes. He's wearing a gray suit I'd love to get my hands on, with a maroon tie, gold cuff links, and the shiniest shoes I've ever seen. The next thing I notice is a definite chill in the room, like somebody just opened a window. He turns to the manager.

"Please make sure our name is never mentioned in connection with this incident."

"Huh?" says the manager. "Yeah, sure."

"Thank you." He shakes the manager's hand, and when he releases his grip, I see a flash of green.

"Come, Kevin," says Mr. Reynolds. He pivots and heads for the door. During the whole time, Mr. Reynolds hasn't once looked at his bloody son.

My dad and I are right behind them. As we follow them out through the lobby, Kevin glances back at me. He doesn't look angry anymore. What he looks is miserable.

Later I'm in my room, sitting on the bed. My dad has delivered a few choice words, plus he's grounded me for a month. I'm staring at the walls, something I'll be seeing a lot of in the next few weeks.

I can't get that look of Kevin's out of my head. The more I think about it, the harder it is for me to call him El Creepo. I wonder what it's like having a father who's so worried about his reputation that he doesn't bother to get mad. I think back to when my father was yelling at me, and it almost makes me smile.

There's a knock on the door, and Nick sticks his head in. "There must be some mistake," he says. "They told me I'd find Mike Tyson in here."

"Yo, Nick. You heard what happened?"

"How many times have I warned you not to take on guys bigger than you are?" he says. "In your case, that means nobody over the age of eight."

"Hey, I had no choice." I give him the whole story, including the part about Kevin's strong-arm tactics. When I finish, he leans back against the wall with a strange smile on his face.

"This Becky, she's some little operator, isn't she?"

"What do you mean?" I ask.

"She held his hand, right? She kissed him first?"

"Well, yeah."

"I got news for you, kiddo. She got what was coming to her."

"Nick, she was scared. He had her pinned to the seat."

"She's a tease."

"What's that?"

94

"You'll find out. There's a million more like her."

He gets up from the bed and walks to the window, where he looks out at the big oak tree in our front yard. "Did I tell you Cindy and I broke up?"

"When did this happen?"

"Last night. I took her to dinner at Mario's, and on the way home she says she's calling it quits. Just like that. Boom."

"How come?"

"That's the crazy part," he says. "I don't know. I mean, I listened to what she said, but it was like she was speaking a foreign language or something."

He looks over at me. "Women are different, Sammy. They're not the same as you and me. Never forget that."

"Hey, they're people," I say.

"You really are just a kid, aren't you?" He ruffles my hair and smiles at me, but all I can see are those sad eyes of his.


Monday during lunch period Gus and I are out on the playground. Every so often somebody comes up and asks me what happened to my eye. I tell them they should see the other guy.

Suddenly I spot Becky and Alice. "Time to make another move," I tell Gus.

"On Alice Biddle?" he says in a sickly voice.

"No, on the Pope."

"Yesterday in the hall she called me Lizard Breath."

"Perfect," I say. "She's already using pet names."

"I don't know, Sammy."

95

"Trust me. She's like putty in your hands."

We wait until the two of them split up. When Alice walks off, Gus gives me this pleading look.

"Putty," I tell him.

He shrugs and slinks off after her. Meanwhile, I hurry after Becky to make a move of my own. I decide on the take-charge approach.

"Okay, here's the deal," I tell her when I catch up.

She just keeps walking. There's something familiar about this scene, but I can't stop to figure it out now. Deciding the take-charge approach was a mistake, I remember something Nick used to say: *Flattery will get you everywhere.*

"Hey, nice shirt," I tell her. She doesn't say a word.

As I rack my brains trying to understand what's wrong, another one of Nick's sayings comes to me: *Act sincere.*

"Becky," I tell her, "I got this special feeing toward you."

She just keeps staring ahead. Finally I can't stand it anymore.

"I don't believe it," I say. "I help you out at the movies and this is the thanks I get?"

She stops and puts her hands on her hips. "Help me out! I've never been so embarrassed in my life."

"I saved you from Kevin Reynolds. Doesn't that mean anything?"

"Sammy, you were following me!"

"Well, okay, but it was for your own good. The way things turned out, you should be glad I was there."

"Get this straight, Sammy Carducci. I don't need you spying on me or butting into my life. I'm not some posses-

96

sion for you to win or lose. And I don't like being a guinea pig for your stupid theories on women."

It's like somebody punched me in the solar plexus. How does she know about my theories? That information is top secret. It could be dangerous in the wrong hands. Hers, for instance.

I realize there's only one way she could have found out. "Gus! I'm gonna break his scrawny neck."

"Don't be ridiculous. He's your best friend."

"Not anymore."

"Sammy," she says, "I tricked him into telling me. Then I used him to trick you."

"Huh?"

"Gus told you where I'd be Friday night, didn't he?"

"Well, yeah."

"I gave him that information on purpose," she says. "I knew he'd take it straight to you."

"You mean you wanted me to follow you?"

"Yes, so I could teach you a lesson. Remember the ice cream shop? Remember the fat woman with the sweater?"

"You knew we were there the whole time!"

She nods. "Dark glasses and all."

Things are moving too fast for me. I have to stop to let my brain catch up. "Wait a second. You saw us sitting behind you in the theater?"

"That's right."

"And you still kissed Kevin Reynolds?"

"Sammy, that's the *reason* I kissed Kevin Reynolds. To make you jealous. It's why I went out with him in the first place."

I stand there with my jaw flapping in the breeze.

"I turned Kevin down the first time he asked me out. The second, third, and fourth time, too. I didn't say yes until after I talked to Gus and learned about your theories."

I feel like an idiot, but I also feel great. Is that possible?

"Are you going out with Kevin again?" I ask.

"I don't think so."

"Because of what he did?"

"Partly," she said. "But the main thing is that he's too old. I'm not a woman, even though I might look like one. I'm a girl. Sometimes I get tired of trying to act like a grown-up, and I just want to play jump rope or tag."

"You mean like this?" I ask, tagging her. She nods, still thinking about what she said.

"Well?" I say. "You're it."

"Don't be silly. We weren't really playing. Because if we were, I would have tagged you first, like this."

"But I tagged you first," I tell her.

"It didn't count."

"Did so."

"Did not."

"Did so."

"Did not."

"Did so."

"Okay," she says, "and I tagged you second. So *you're* it."

She takes off across the playground, with me right behind her. Just as I'm about to catch up, she throws a wicked head fake, and suddenly Alice Biddle is straight ahead. Over to one side, Gus is shuffling away sadly. Obviously, Alice has just shot him down.

"You're it!" I yell to Alice, digging at her ribs.

She jumps, then looks back and glares at me. "If you're trying to lure me into some childish game, you can just forget it."

"Fine," I tell her. "Then you'll be it all day, with whatever cooties that involves."

She pretends to walk off, but as she passes Gus, she touches his shoulder. "You're it!" she says, then runs away.

He goes after her, then she chases me, then I chase Becky around and around the playground, past the tetherball pole and jungle gym and sandbox. By the time I tag her, she's grinning and so am I.

"Hey, Sammy," she says, "your tie is loose."

All of a sudden, as I glance down at myself, my clothes look funny. What's an eleven-year-old doing in a suit, anyway? What am I trying to prove? Maybe I should wear jeans and a T-shirt instead. Maybe I should give up spaghetti and start eating peanut butter sandwiches. Maybe I should get rid of the breath mints and the pocket comb and the nose-hair scissors. Maybe it's time I stopped trying to be so different and started acting like a normal kid.

Nah.

# ABOUT THE AUTHOR

Author RONALD KIDD says: "When I was in the sixth grade, I kissed a girl for the first time. She was gigantic. I remember kind of holding her by the elbows and standing on my tiptoes so I could peck her on the cheek. I didn't know what else to do because none of the love stories I'd read had covered the topic of romance between a shrimp and a giant.

"Years later, I decided to remedy the situation. Somehow the shrimp, Sammy Carducci, took over the story. He made me laugh. I hope he does the same for you. Just don't take his advice."

Ronald Kidd lives with his wife in Nashville, Tennessee. He is the author of several popular books for young readers, including *Sizzle and Splat* and *Second Fiddle*.